her scottish ceo

Her Scottish CEO
Written and Illustrated
by Christy Olesen

Indie-Pendent Publishing Co.
http://www.indie-pendentpublishing.com

For Mom, my best friend and confidant.

And Dely, for your continued support and encouragement.

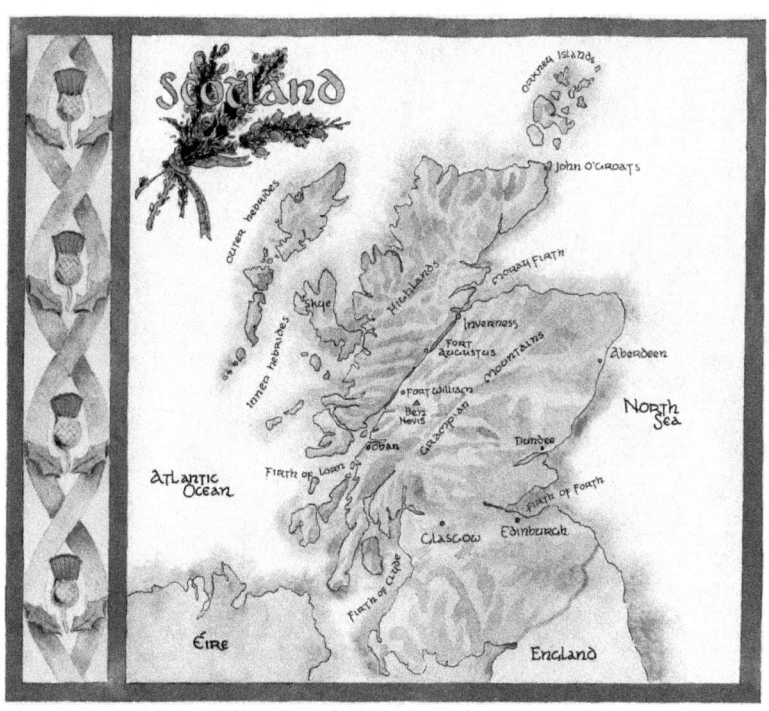

Map of Scotland showing the Great Glen

some journeys are only beginning when you arrive.

Gaelic Saying

Ben Nevis, Britain's tallest mountain at 4,406 ft. The towns of Coal, Inverlochy and Fort William sit at its base along the shores of Loch Linnhe

CHAPTER ONE

"*Och*, lass, watch yerself!" The Scot's accent rang in Marcie Winter's ear, two big hands clamped on her shoulders as momentum carried them both full circle. Her shoulder bag was knocked to the ground before the man disappeared into the morning crowd. At least he hadn't snatched it.

"Oh, my paintings!" Horrified, Marcie dropped to her knees to retrieve her bag and its contents. Small watercolor paintings, pencils, brushes, lipgloss, postcards and keys littered the sidewalk around her. She could see her hard work about to be trampled by tourists' feet, and scrambled to retrieve her illustrations before they were damaged.

A man crouched beside her and grabbed the ones beyond her reach. He wore a fine charcoal business jacket paired with a blue and green kilt. Marcie had seen several men in kilts in the week she'd been in the Highlands, but never for the office. He was quite striking and made her wish she'd worn her sundress instead of jeans.

9

While he studied her artwork, she studied him. Even folded up, she could tell he was tall. His wavy, burnt-ochre hair reminded her of Joel. She wondered if he had dreamy, chocolate-brown eyes like Joel's. Homesickness and a stab of anger caught her unaware. She must have sighed because the man looked up, concerned.

No, he didn't resemble Joel. His eyes were as green as the verdurous hills around Fort William. Bright, intelligent, curious. An unsettling connection startled her as his eyes trapped hers. He looked at her as though he knew her. Then a sad, desolate emotion changed his expression from that of a kind stranger to one of an anguished soul. It passed in a heartbeat and he looked away, back to her artwork in his hands. But she'd seen it, and she knew he hadn't wanted her to see it. And she wondered why. Why had he looked at her as if he'd known her? Then as if he'd lost her?

She continued to observe him as he looked at her artwork. He had a straight nose and an average mouth, which, with his green eyes, came together to make him *the* most handsome man she'd ever seen.

Up close and personal-wise.

Concentrate, breathe. Don't look stunned.

She reached to gather her pencils and brushes, and composure.

"Oban, nicely done." He handed her the painting of the coastal town. "No damage." Then he smiled. The smile was just a little tug at the corners of his mouth as though he were unaccustomed to smiling or unwilling or just didn't have the heart. Bittersweet, it made her want to know what was holding his full smile in check. Even so, the smile made her heart skip, her pulse accelerate.

She took the watercolors and smiled back with no reserve. "Thanks for your help."

He stood but didn't leave.

With the watercolors safe in her bag, she picked up her lip gloss, sunglasses and bug spray, then examined her camera. Satisfied it was undamaged, she closed her bag and began to rise.

"Are you a'right, lassie?" He took her arm to assist her, his touch firm, gentle and… *impersonal.*

her scottish ceo

At five-foot-seven, Marcie's eyes were even with the knot in his beautiful blue and green tartan tie, a perfect match to his kilt. She looked up. "Yes, I'm fine. I guess I wasn't paying attention to where I was going."

"Have you drawn anything here in Fort William?"

"Just some vignettes. I only arrived last evening." She held out the watercolors she'd done that morning in the neighborhood of her bed and breakfast, illustrations of quaint cottages with tile roofs, climbing roses and lace curtains. He took them carefully, obviously appreciating their value to her.

"I know this neighborhood." He shuffled through the vignettes, then stopped to examine one. "My good friends recently purchased this house. Is this one for sale? It would make a brilliant housewarming gift." He looked at her expectantly.

Should she sell it? It was part of the collection she was under contract to produce. Her contract was for sixty full illustrations of Scotland's Great Glen, from Oban to Inverness, and as many small vignettes as she wanted to add. However, as long as she handed in sixty watercolor illustrations at the end of her six weeks in Scotland, she would have fulfilled her contract.

It would be wonderful to know the owners of the house would hang her work on their wall. "I adore that cottage. It's just a few houses from the bed and breakfast where I'm staying."

The man looked at his watch, then said something under his breath that sounded Gaelic. Then, "Sorry, I'm late." He handed her the vignettes. Had she lost the sale that quickly? She could use the extra cash, maybe even buy a new cell phone. "Can I have your number?" he continued. "We'll arrange to meet and I can purchase it then."

Marcie searched her bag for one of the cards she'd picked up in the lobby of the bed and breakfast, but everything was jumbled.

The most handsome man she'd ever met—*up close and personal-wise*—handed her a card and said words that made her wonder if she was dreaming. "Call me. After one o'clock. Right now, I have an appointment to keep." He held out his hand. "Name's Greg."

"Marcie." She took his hand. It enveloped hers in a warm, strong grip, and she felt that sensation of connection again. She

11

hadn't imagined it. Neither of them let go for several seconds, and even as he backed away, his fingers lingered, their fingertips touching for a moment longer.

Then he smiled. Full force. Just the way she'd hoped he could. Add the sparkle in his eyes and she was a goner.

He turned and walked up High Street. A limp made her wonder if her heavy camera had landed on his foot. He must have been right behind the man who had bumped into her, close enough to have been hit by the fallout.

Her artist's eye appreciated his broad shoulders and long legs, and she thought he might be more comfortable in outdoor gear than the clothing he wore. Chewing her thumbnail, she watched as he stopped before a building across the street from where she'd parked her rental car. He turned, lifted his hand, then disappeared into the doorway.

Her heart still pounding, she sighed, turned and continued on her way. He could make her forget Joel.

Joel who?

***

Gregor McInnis VI climbed the stairs two at a time to reach the well-furnished office on the top floor. The secretary's desk was vacant. He stopped to tug at his tie and check that his handkerchief was folded and tucked in just right. He adjusted his sporran, the pouch worn in front of his kilt, then went in unannounced. He was expected.

And he was late, would have been late even if he hadn't stopped to help Marcie. He sat in a leather chair in front of a polished walnut desk. Across the desk sat an older version of himself, talking on the phone but eyeing his grandson. Greg could tell his grandfather was annoyed.

He shifted and rubbed his hipbone.

Greg's grandfather, Gregor McInnis IV, replaced the phone and drilled his grandson with a disapproving look Greg was more than familiar with. "Another climbing accident? Or a game of shinty?"

"Neither, sir, a collision with a zoom lens, just a bruise." Greg straightened, ready for the inevitable conference. All visits with his grandfather were conferences, not conversations.

The phone buzzed and Old Gregor picked it up.

Greg sighed. This meeting could take forever without Ms. Moore at her desk to screen the calls.

He turned his mind to Marcie. An ordinary person, dressed in blue jeans and a T-shirt, a raincoat tied around her waist, an American accent. He wouldn't have noticed her had he not nearly tripped over her as she knelt to pick up her belongings. She was such a strong reminder of Emma that it had almost knocked him off balance as he'd crouched on the sidewalk to help. Then Marcie had flashed a radiant smile that had made him want to fall into it and soak up her happiness. Her eyes, sparkling blue, had been wide open, as though she always looked at the world in wonder. Her straight, golden hair swung evenly, brushing her shoulders as she moved. He had thought simple beauty would never affect him again, but he was wrong. She had captivated him.

Finished with his phone conversation, Old Gregor pulled a book from the credenza behind him and tossed it across the desk to land before his grandson. "Explain this!"

Greg didn't need to look at it; he knew it well. "It's an outstanding book. Reviews have called it brilliant. Sales at the book fair far exceeded expectations. Orders are pouring in."

"I'm not talking about sales. I expressly forbade this book to be produced."

"As CEO I can authorize any book I feel has merit."

"Even as *interim* CEO your authority still comes from me. I *am* the publisher here. How is it I knew nothing about this until now? How did it get through production without my knowledge?"

Greg shrugged his shoulders and didn't look Old Gregor in the eye. It had taken all his best people to pull this off without the firm's patriarch knowing. But Greg had known the old man would find out soon enough. He felt just a little smug that his grandfather hadn't found out until the book *Himalayan Odyssey* was off the press. Two years in the making and the old man hadn't had a clue. Greg had been hoping his grandfather would find the book worth the secrecy. That he would commend Greg for a job well done. Unfortunately, at the moment he didn't see that reaction in his grandfather's wise old eyes.

"I forbade this project because of the danger involved."

"It has been my project since… I'm here. I was in no danger." He felt a tug of guilt at the lie. Just one of many he'd told in the last few years.

"You could at least have gotten someone else to do it. You haven't changed much from your obstreperous youth, have you? I had hoped the responsibility of the job would settle you. You need some maturity."

Maturity? He'd organized an expedition that had produced the *Himalayan Odyssey*. Hadn't that been enough to prove he *had* settled to the job, that he *had* grown up? All his life only his father had seen promise in Greg's limitless energy—traveling the world to photograph uncommon and wild landscapes—as an asset to the firm. Greg's grandfather and uncle had expressed doubts about his ability to take over for his father. It seemed they still had them. Without his father to defend him, Greg was feeling alone on his side of the fence. He needed to prove to his grandfather—and maybe to himself—that he could do the job he'd been dropped into when his father had died unexpectedly.

Old Gregor reached across the desk and opened the book to a double-page spread with a startling photograph. He poked a knobby finger at the image. "How can you say photographing a blizzard on Mount Everest is not dangerous? And a casualty! For the first time in the history of McInnis House Press, a casualty—"

"Third time."

"I'm not counting your father or McCulluah. They were not employees. For God's sake, we're book publishers, not a bunch of oil riggers." He sat back, sagged a bit and looked older.

Greg's smugness evaporated as he looked at his grandfather.

"Greg, promise me, as long as I'm alive at least, you'll never pull a stunt like this again. I lost my son, I will not outlive my grandson." The old man looked away.

Greg knew emotion did not sit well with his grandfather. It was a trait he'd inherited himself. "I'm sorry if I upset you. It was something I had to do. I have no plans to repeat it. In fact, I plan to concentrate on business and limit my photography to the Highlands." His lust for adventure had been ripped from him in that blizzard.

14

The phone's intercom buzzed and his grandfather took the call.

Greg picked up the book and turned the page. It creaked as the new, stiff binding gave way. The glossy pages felt like ice. An involuntary shiver vibrated through him. The ink's faint chemical scent wafted off the new pages but did not push away the painful images brought to mind. He had no doubt the fear, the nightmare, would invade his life for years to come. Not because he had been in danger, but because he had put the entire team, the support team that included his best friends, in danger. And Emma. It was still hard to think about Emma.

The photographs weren't his father's, as originally planned, they'd been lost with him. But Greg's humble effort to recapture his father's vision had been a success to all but him. He knew in his heart that his father's lost photographs would have made a better book.

The expedition's outcome lay open in his hands. Cold, heavy, *done*. And he had no appetite to attempt it ever again.

When his grandfather was off the phone, Greg closed the book and put it into his outstretched, crinkled hand. The old man put the book back on the credenza and turned a kinder face to his grandson. "I'm sorry, son. I can see you had feelings for the girl. I didn't know."

His grandfather's apology stunned and touched Greg. Two reminders of Emma in one morning. It was almost enough to shatter his equilibrium. He thought he'd shut the door on that emotional storm months ago, but here it was, blasting open, colder than ever.

It took a moment before he could speak as he worked the ice from his throat. "She was an excellent photographer. It was a waste."

She was my wife.

The memories, the guilt, the pain moved in through that reopened door behind which he'd thought he'd banished them forever. He'd been unable to deal with their existence then. Could he now?

"Any life cut short is a waste, which is why I forbade this endeavor three years ago when your father insisted on *his* odyssey."

"Dad's trip into the Himalayas was successful. It was a faulty carburetor in that rattletrap plane that killed him."

"You're so like your father, always bent on some adventure." Old Gregor shifted, uneasy. "You didn't break your foot playing rugby in Barbados two years ago, did you? You weren't in Barbados."

Greg felt wretched as the lies he'd told rolled over him. The displeasure in his grandfather's eyes made him feel even worse. He'd told the lies to save his grandfather from worry and to guarantee the expedition wouldn't be stopped, but he hadn't expected this vehement reaction. Sure, he'd known his grandfather would rant, but he'd expected that afterward he would accept Greg's decisions as good for business. "No, sir. I wasn't in Barbados."

At the time it had seemed vitally important to fulfill his father's dream to photograph the Himalayas. He'd had a single-minded compulsion to do it, whatever the cost. But the cost had been too high. And that's all his grandfather saw. He didn't see the spectacular photographs his team had produced. He didn't see the potential for awards and sales and accolades.

"You broke your foot on Everest, in that blizzard."

"No, sir. I didn't break my foot." He hesitated. His grandfather waited, expecting clarification. "Frostbite. I lost a few toes on my left foot."

"*Damnadh!* That's why you still limp. You'll never recover from that. The others?"

"Frostbite affected us all. Others worse than I was."

"And the girl?"

"Legal can give you a report." Again, Greg couldn't look his grandfather in the eye. He couldn't speak of Emma. Not yet. Maybe never.

"I'm sorry, Son. I'm sorry you were injured. I'm sorry the girl died. I'm sorry you felt you had to do this without my consent or knowledge. And I'm disappointed you felt you had to lie to me."

"I apologize, Granddad." He felt duly chastised and remorseful. "It was important at the time."

"I suppose it's understandable, after what happened to your father. I guess we're lucky the girl's family didn't bring suit against us."

"She had no family." He'd wanted to give her family. He'd wanted to give her the world.

"Your hotel is comfortable?"

Greg was relieved his grandfather changed the subject. "I'm staying with Uncle Rowan and Aunt Madeline."

"Aye, of course. Why they wanted to build such a huge house, I don't know. The family home, *Mòirneas,* will be theirs in a few years, if not sooner. Unless you've changed your mind?"

"No, I'm happy at the Inverness townhouse. I'm actually enjoying the reno, despite the disruption and chaos. No, *Mòirneas* is too big for one. Besides, you'll be there for decades."

"*Och,* no! I'm eighty-three!" The old man scrunched up his face and pointed a crooked finger at Greg. "And you're thirty-three. It's time you married and settled down."

Greg had never told his grandfather about Emma, that they'd married on a whim in Nepal and she'd died in that blizzard on the mountain before their first month as husband and wife had passed. It was all caught up in the lies he'd told to shelter his grandfather, to protect his mission, to protect his heart.

He'd made mistakes. The biggest mistakes in his life. Maybe he wasn't ready to take over for his father.

His grandfather continued. "I was married with two children by your age, so was your father. What's that bonnie lass's name? You know, McCalluah's daughter."

"Courtney."

"Marry her. She's right for you. You've known her for years. Her father left her well off, didn't he? She's from an old Scottish family."

Greg didn't answer. He knew what came next.

"You need an heir. McInnis House needs an heir. She'll make you a good wife. She can run your house, host parties for your business associates. If I remember, she's on the skinny side. By the time she's had a few bairns she'll have filled out nicely. She's tall, too."

Once more his grandfather turned away to answer the intercom's buzz; his finger was always on the pulse of the business.

Greg was relieved; he wasn't going *there* again.

***

Marcie shaded her eyes with her city guide as she looked up at the brilliant, cloudless sky. The day would be hot. It was unusual for the air to be so heavy with humidity yet lack the usual rain, clouds, or wind. Tourists on Fort William's streets had shed their windbreakers and donned their sunglasses as they hurried off to museums, mountain hikes or just to stroll the streets.

It didn't take Marcie long to find the library. She wanted to check her email, then get back to painting. It was why she had been in a hurry and hadn't paid attention when she'd rounded the corner and bumped into that man.

```
Hi Marcie,
     Sorry you lost your cell phone. It
probably wouldn't work over there anyway.
There's a vacancy in the art dept. at the
middle school. You'll have to get here before
the end of June to secure the job.
     Dad

     Hi Dad,
     My current job won't end until the
first of July. As I've said before, I'm an
illustrator, not a teacher.
       Marcie
     Hey Marcie.
     I ran into Joel yesterday when I helped
with the faculty physicals. He sure keeps fit
for a man his age. He told me you're in
Scotland. Scotland? I always told you to step
out of your comfort zone. Well, you sure did!
You stepped right into the Highlands.
U*GO*GIRL!
     Joel also said you've broken up. I'm so
sorry, but really, I always thought you could
do better — and younger. I don't mean he
wasn't right for you at the time, but you're
the girl who deserves the Happy Ever After.
```

Career, family, devoted man, the whole
package!
    Let me know what's happening. I wish
you great success — you deserve it.
    Wallis.
    P.S. Seen any dishy men in kilts? Do
tell!

    Hi Wallie!
    Yes, I stepped out of my comfort zone,
and boy, was it a big step — 7,000 miles.
I'll be here six weeks total; five days have
already slipped by. It's beautiful, I love
it!
    I'm glad Joel is well, though I
wouldn't feel too guilty wishing him a raging
case of athlete's foot or maybe some mid-life
baldness to go with his mid-life crisis.
    Yes, I've seen a few men in kilts,
mostly near the tourist sites playing
bagpipes. But today! Get this! I met the most
handsome man ever. Sigh… Just to be that
close to a perfect specimen was a thrill. My
heart palpitates just remembering him. He
wore a beautiful blue/green tartan kilt.
Sigh… And he has a heavenly Scottish accent.
Enough brogue to know he's from the
Highlands, but not so thick that I can't
understand him. I might see him again. He
wants to buy one of my vignettes!
    Bye-bye.
    Marcie.

Marcie had hoped to see an email from Joel. Hoped, but
hadn't expected it. It was over. He was probably already dipping
into the ever-flowing stream of co-ed art students that sluiced
through his studio and his life. They were his fountain of youth.
Joel collected protégées the way some men collected car parts. He
tinkered with them, got them working, then moved on.

He'd got her working, given her the key and let her run at
full throttle.

He'd always promised to get her an appointment with
Amanda Roth, *the* most successful art-licensing agent in the

country, maybe the world. With licensing, Marcie would get royalties for every greeting card, calendar, mug or T-shirt that sold with one of her images on it. Ms. Roth had an unsurpassed reputation for catapulting talented artists to the top in the illustration and design industry. But the appointment had never happened. And now that Joel had dropped her, it probably never would. Another disappointment in a long string of disappointments she was determined to end. Setting her jaw, Marcie vowed she would get an appointment on her own. It would be harder without Joel's recommendation, but she could do it, would do it.

Joel had bolstered her ego until she could see *financially successful artist* following her name, but he hadn't followed through.

He never committed. That was his problem. He always thought there might be something better, someone better, just around the corner. That thought reminded her of Greg, how he'd helped her that morning. Maybe it was an omen; maybe there was something better, someone better for her. *Just around the corner.*

***

Marcie looked at her watch; three more hours until she could call Greg. It was going to be a long morning. She walked back to where she had left her rented car, eager to get to her next location.

Standing in her rental car's open door, she looked up at the building Greg had disappeared into an hour ago and searched the windows.

***

Greg stood. Sitting, waiting, was difficult if his mind wasn't occupied with something worthwhile. It wasted time, and you never knew how much time you had. He crossed his grandfather's office, passed floor to ceiling bookcases containing almost every important book published in the last five generations of McInnis House Press, to a window overlooking Loch Linnhe. The heavy air veiled the Ardgour and Kingairloch hills beyond the estuary, their greens were not so bright, their formations not so defined. It would be difficult to photograph, but would make an arresting image.

At a car park across the street, at the estuary's edge, someone caught his eye. Marcie? He shifted closer to the window to get a better look. Yes. She approached a green Rover salon. As she opened the door she turned and looked up at the building, scanned the windows and stopped at the one where he stood. She waved. He lifted a hand, then let it drop. When she smiled he wanted to be there, with her.

He watched as she got into the car, backed from the parking space then drove the wrong way to the exit. He held his breath when she pulled into traffic and didn't let it go until he was sure she stayed on the left. Tourists. Some always forgot to drive on the left. But she wasn't a tourist. She was here for a purpose: to paint. And she was damn good at it.

Her watercolors had captivated him. In fact, they were exactly what he'd been hoping to find. He smiled as things began to fall in place. He'd been looking for something different to start his new line of local guide books. He'd never have expected to find it on the streets of Fort William, and by accident, not after all the online illustration directories he'd searched. For the first time in a long while he felt excited about something. It felt good.

When his grandfather finished the call, Greg returned to his seat. "I have an idea for something new and exciting. A new direction for McInnis House Press." He wouldn't let the fact that his grandfather had confronted him about the *Himalayan Odyssey* intimidate him.

Old Gregor cocked his head. "Go ahead. Let's hear it."

"I'm working on a series of guide books illustrated with paintings." It was something Greg had worked on for over a year, something exciting and different he'd started to take his mind off the way he'd failed the expedition team, especially Emma. He'd worked hard on his proposal, but until now the vision had been foggy. Today it was sharp and clear. He knew he was taking a chance speaking of it now, but he wanted his grandfather to know he had his mind on the business, that he was thinking ahead, thinking creatively. He needed to prove to his grandfather that he was as good behind the desk as he was behind the camera.

"Greg, you ken as well as I do that McInnis House Press publishes only photographic illustration, and has done so since my grandfather founded the company with an old hand press and a wet-plate camera. It's what we're known for. Why do you want to deviate from what has worked so well for us for over a hundred and fifty years?"

"I have a presentation prepared, I ask only that you consider it."

Old Gregor gave his grandson *the look.* "Considering your past—let us say—exercises in publishing, I've been thinking we dropped you into your father's place too soon. You're more mature now than you were when you took over Ian's position, but not as mature as you need to be to do the job without some supervision or accountability. I feel I need to issue an ultimatum here. Bowl me over with your presentation, within four weeks, or Rowan runs the Inverness office until you're ready to take over."

Greg was stunned. His grandfather was threatening him? Do it right or lose his job? He wasn't a kid. What could he do to make his grandfather see that? Or would he always be swimming up stream? He should just walk out and go back to being the McInnis House Press top photographer. He sighed. Since Emma died, his heart just wasn't in it like it had been when he'd been that carefree, reckless *photog* trekking around the word doing what he did best: capturing the wild, turbulent places on earth.

Since his father died, since Emma died, his life had changed so much from what he'd planned and expected it to be, he was still reeling.

It had always been family tradition that he'd take over for his father. They just hadn't imagined it would be so soon, under such trying conditions. He agreed he still had much to learn, but he thought he'd done well so far for a fish out of water.

He cleared the irritation from his throat and prepared to defend himself. "I understand your annoyance about the Himalaya expedition, but otherwise—"

"The children's Loch Ness Monster coloring book."

Oh, right. Greg had conveniently forgotten that one. The paper choice had been a mistake, it wouldn't take a mark from a basic crayon.

"We daena deal in myths at McInnis House Press. Our lines are based on fact. The Loch Ness Monster is a myth. I've heard no end of jokes from our competitors still, twa years later. Then there's the—"

"I accept your ultimatum." Greg decided he didn't need a list of his managerial failures. He believed in his new idea; he believed it would make up for his learning mistakes and make his grandfather proud. Show his grandfather he *was* mature.

He wanted to keep his job. It was more than a job; it was his heritage, his life.

***

In Corpach, outside Fort William, Marcie parked her car and walked along the old embankment separating the Caledonian Canal entrance from the Loch Linnhe estuary. She watched as a lock closed and filled with water. A small canal boat floated lazily as its captain waited his turn to exit the canal.

The afternoon was sultry, something she hadn't expected in the Highlands. She put on her sunglasses, sat on the grass and took out her paper, pencils and paints. The oppressive humidity and thick atmosphere diminished her view, but there was no wind to struggle with while she painted Ben Nevis, which loomed over Fort William like the hump of a great green whale.

As she studied the scene she let her mind wander. Greg had been at the top of her thoughts all morning. She'd spotted him in the window looking down at her and it had given her a thrill. Still did. At least, she hoped it had been him, the reflections on the glass had made it hard to tell. It was the building she'd seen him walk into and she was sure he'd waved back.

Gulls called each other across the loch and she watched as they swooped and dipped at the water's surface after some morsel only they could see. The dark, peat-stained water lapped at the rocky seawall. The chug of a steam train grew louder as it passed just out of sight, distracting her when she should be painting the tallest mountain in Great Britain.

To be honest, she was already distracted, and would be until it was time to call Greg. Nervous excitement and a little anxiety caused her insides to flutter as she thought about seeing him again. She'd take more of her watercolors and hopefully he'd spend some time studying them. That would give her more time to study him, commit him to memory for future reference. Maybe he'd purchase a watercolor for himself; then she'd always have that connection with him. Connection. She'd felt it the first time she'd looked into his searching eyes.

chRisty olesen

He seemed to have an appreciation for art. A regular passerby would have made more general comments, such as "I've been there, you know, and there's a wonderful tea shop just around the corner." Or "I could never paint like that. Why, I can't even draw a straight line." She had heard them all. She wasn't embarrassed or shy to sit in public and paint. She enjoyed people's comments, especially children's imaginative questions. But Greg had simply said, "Oban, very well done."

She wondered why he'd looked so forlorn.

***

After Greg said goodbye to his grandfather he headed downstairs to the second meeting he had come to Fort William to attend.

"I'm glad to see everyone here." Rowan Tucker, Greg's uncle, grimaced at the lighthearted moans and grunts that rose from the staff. "We're here to brainstorm new ideas for the coming production year. Those of you who have been through this know what's said here stays here. Those of you who are new, this is the list that will be on the shelves in eighteen to twenty-four months." He turned to his nephew. "We'll start with idea generations. Greg, go ahead and start us off."

Greg was sure Rowan thought he would freeze, be unable to come up with any new suggestions without time to prepare. Of course, it was the opening he'd wanted. It was his plan to get the reaction of the editorial and design staff now, so he'd be better prepared to counter their concerns when he gave his full proposal. "I have an idea for a guide book featuring Fort William—"

"It's been done a thousand times," one editor said. "And a dozen times by us, no less, the last one only a year ago. It's too soon."

"I was thinking along different lines." Greg sat back in his chair and stretched his long legs, crossed at the ankles, under the table. A breeze from the oscillating fan in the corner lifted his kilt just enough to tickle the hairs on his thighs. "A series, starting with the Fort William and the Lochaber area. An illustrated book, a journal/guidebook, watercolors most likely, though other mediums will be considered."

"Now Greg, you know very well McInnis House Press is known for its photographic illustrations." Uncle Rowan was in a

24

snippy mood. But it was true, as Old Gregor had said, Greg's great-great-grandfather's talent with the new medium of photography had made MHP a thriving business. But it was the ruthless glint in Rowan's eyes that alerted Greg: the man wanted Greg to fail. He wanted Greg's job, because eventually he wanted Old Gregor's job. That would never happen if Greg could help it. Rowan Tucker wasn't a McInnis; he'd married Greg's father's sister. There had always been a McInnis as head of the business. Greg wanted it to stay that way as long as possible. *Och*, there was that heir problem nudging him again, but that was in the future. First he had to secure his job, his place in the family business.

"There's always room for change, always room for growth," Greg said with steel in his voice. He was glad to see Rowan flinch.

Now he just needed Marcie to call him. With his offer to buy the watercolor, he knew she would. He could tell she would welcome the money. If the bed and breakfast she was staying in was near his friends' cottage, then it was one of the more economic hostelries in Fort William. It was in a neighborhood of older homes where older couples and widows opened their homes to supplement their pensions. Younger couples, like his friends, and entrepreneurs were moving in, restoring the homes and upgrading the bed and breakfast inns, but the area was still a bit depressed. It bothered him some that she was staying in that area. She was probably safe enough, but he'd rather see her in one of the nicer neighborhoods.

He couldn't get caught up in her welfare now. He had no idea yet if she could do—or would want to do—his project. But his gut feeling was that she would. He could see the same eagerness in her eyes, hear the same excitement in her voice, when she talked about her artwork that he felt for his project.

In her hands ordinary, everyday objects and scenes lost their mundane, taken-for-granted existence and were placed, for a moment in time, in a position of honor, a new concept for him. He'd always tried to find the extraordinary and exotic. The fact that he could use his lenses and filters to make common objects uncommon, had never interested him.

He wanted to see more of her work. Already his mind raced ahead to calendars, T-shirts, cards and mugs; her work was perfect for MHP's licensing program.

He needed *new* and *fresh* in his work. Today he'd found it.

***

When the meeting was over at noon the group walked to a nearby restaurant. Greg scanned the passersby, hoping to see Marcie. He should have waited for her to give him her number, but knowing how his grandfather insisted on punctuality, he hadn't had the nerve to make the old man wait any longer. He looked at his watch and hoped the lunch wouldn't last over an hour. If she didn't call, he'd knock on every bed and breakfast on that street until he found her. His proposal would be uninspired without her art.

He needed her to keep his position in his family's business.

The Ardgour hills across Loch Linnhe

CHAPTER TWO

Marcie breathed deeply as a cooling breeze blew in from the West. The hot morning eased and now typical Highland clouds chased each other across the sky, first taking and then spilling the light. Marcie decided to spend the afternoon sketching people, and the best place for that was a park. But first she had to call Greg. The first pay phone she came to had been vandalized. She searched and found another, deposited some coins and called the first number on the card he'd given her.

"Mr. McInnis' office." It was a woman's voice. Marcie was disappointed.

"Is Greg available?"

"I'm sorry, he's in a meeting and cannot be disturbed. May I take a message?"

"Yes. Tell him Marcie called and that I will be in the park until six."

"Uh, which park?"

"The Parade in city center."

chRisty olesen

"I'll give him the message as soon as he checks in. Anything else?"

"Please tell him he can reach me at Mrs. Scott's bed and breakfast after six. Thanks." Marcie hung up the phone feeling desolate. He was probably too busy to meet her. Maybe he'd already forgotten her and the watercolor he'd wanted to buy. She didn't care about selling the painting so much, she just wanted to see him again.

She put more coins in the pay phone and dialed the next number, but this time nothing happened. The phone was dead. Seldom used, she guessed pay phone maintenance wasn't a priority. Losing her cell phone her first day in Scotland might be the stupidest thing she'd ever done.

Her elation of the morning faded as she walked to Fort William's city center. There were more than a few possible subjects on the Parade—the city park or town square. She sat on a bench, talked herself back into the mood, and started to sketch. Wind blew across the grass and tugged at her paper. She took more bankers' clips from her bag and clipped her paper to the hard plastic sheet she used as a drawing board. It wasn't easy to work in the wind but she loved painting outdoors: warm sun, cool wind, scents of grass and sea with people going about their daily routines. *En plein air* they had called it in college. She just called it *plain fun.*

She finished a difficult vignette of children kicking a ball and looked around for a more stationary subject. A man sat on a bench to her left. He hadn't been there a moment ago but now she had a good view of him. If he'd sit still for two minutes she'd have a good sketch. He struggled to keep the newspaper upright in the wind. He'd stretched his long, jean-clad legs straight out and crossed them at the ankle. A scruffy black dog lay at his feet with its head on its paws.

Her sketch done, she started to fill in the details. Looking more closely, she realized who it was and caught her breath. A thrill fluttered through her. His casual clothes—light windbreaker and worn blue jeans—were the reason she hadn't recognized him at first.

Smiling, feeling the excitement return, she finished the sketch and dabbed on splashes of color. She couldn't capture the glint in his green eyes or the sun reflecting off his hair as the wind tussled it. If she were closer, she'd be very tempted to run her fingers through it. Nor could she capture the scents she remembered from their first meeting—sun-warmed skin and woodsy cologne. Nor could she capture his voice, which was as deep and caressing as the hypnotic bodhrán, a drum she'd heard Celtic folksingers play. But this one would be a keeper. It would remind her of the feelings of discovery and excitement she'd experienced meeting him.

It had only been a couple of weeks since Joel had dumped her. Was she really so fickle as to be fantasizing out another man? But he wasn't just any man. He was *the* most handsome man she'd ever met, as well as being kind and considerate. That was a quick judgement so soon after meeting him, but she felt in her heart she was right.

When she looked up, his newspaper was folded and one arm lay casually across the back of the bench. He was watching her. She smiled, waved. He hadn't forgotten her; he'd received her message and had come to meet her. Or maybe just to buy the painting.

Greg rose, handed his newspaper to an old man passing by, and came to stand at her shoulder. The little dog followed. Marcie's pulse quickened.

She put down her brush and looked up at him. "Hello again."

He stood with his hands in his back pockets, his jacket open to a black T-shirt stretched across a well-defined chest. She was right: he looked good in casual clothes. Really good. He looked younger, more carefree, even reckless if that could be summed up in the few feet he'd covered walking over to her.

"I didn't want to disturb you while you were working. You don't mind if I watch?"

"Not at all. I'm used to people watching me."

"I'd like to see what you've painted today."

She was disappointed. He'd come to see her work, not her. It was a nice fantasy, anyway.

He sat beside her on the bench. "I should introduce myself properly. Greg McInnis, Inverness."

"Marcie Winters, San Francisco recently, but originally from Center City, Nevada."

"Nice to meet you, Marcie. This is Bobby." He picked up the dog, set it on his knees and scratched its head.

"Like Grayfriars Bobby." She held out a fist for the little dog to sniff. "He looks like him."

"Aye. I found him in Grayfriars, so Bobby it had to be."

"He's perfect." She ran her fingers over the little terrier's silky ears.

"Do you have your work on a web site where I can view it? Or with an agency I can contact?"

Stunned he was that interested in her work, she fumbled in her bag then handed him a card. "This is the university web site with my gallery link on the back." She also handed him the vignettes she'd done and took Bobby onto her own lap.

Since childhood, people had been impressed with her artwork, from the crayon drawings she'd done before she started school to the masterworks she'd completed as a postgraduate. People marveled at her talent, envied her, called her remarkable, talented, gifted. A prodigy. Opinions she hadn't heard from her parents who had little use for her *silly pastime*. They were scholars and disappointed she hadn't pursued academics. Her father had eventually acknowledged her desire to work in the arts, though he thought she'd be more secure as an art teacher with a steady job.

She didn't want Greg to notice her art. She wanted him to notice *her*. She wasn't beautiful, but some said she was pretty. She thought she was just ordinary, everyday, but with a lot to offer.

"These are brilliant." Greg took time to look closely at each one. "This child with the ball is enchanting. The lamppost with the flower baskets—amazing detail. Ah, you've caught me relaxing with the newspaper. There are people who would pay a few quid to see this. And you've captured Bobby well. The wee smatchet is chewing on my shoelace!" He looked through the sheets again before handing them back to her and taking Bobby. "I'm looking for artists for new projects. Would you be interested?"

"Oh, that's exciting." Marcie had no idea if her current job would lead to another with the same company, so it would be good to have another connection. "Right now I'm working for a publisher in Glasgow. When I'm finished, I'd like to learn more about your projects."

"Who is the publisher? Maybe I know someone there."

"Caledon and Bishops. Mr. Fairmont is the project director."

"I know Caledon, but I've never met Mr. Fairmont. When will you finish?"

"I leave Scotland the end of June." She didn't want to think of that now. Not when she'd just met the most exciting man ever, a man she wanted to know better, spend more time with. He didn't look like the businessman she'd met that morning. Now, in jeans and a T-shirt he looked younger, his eyes sparkled with mischief. His wind tousled hair made him look reckless, and there was some bad boy thrown in just to put her off balance. She cleared her throat and tried not to squeak. "Who do you work for?"

"McInnis House Press. We're a small local house. We do travel guides and educational material."

"McInnis? It's your business?" That was impressive.

"My family's business. Don't let me stop you from working. I'd like to watch."

She did two more vignettes: some teenage backpackers sitting on the grass; an older couple sitting companionably on a bench opposite, each reading a section of Greg's donated newspaper.

They talked easily, in generalities, as new acquaintances do. Even with Joel, she'd never felt this comfortable, this companionable. Greg seemed tuned to her thoughts; he wasn't mentally off somewhere else. She asked her fill of questions about the Western Highlands. She could hear the pride in his voice as he spoke about his homeland. The underlying sadness she'd noticed that morning had lifted. She hoped she had some part in helping him forget whatever it was that had shadowed his day.

When she finished the second illustration, Greg put Bobby on the grass. "May I see the cottage painting?"

"Yes, here." She handed it to him.

"What's the price?"

"Since I'm doing it as part of my job, I'm not sure. But since you know the owners of the house, I would like them to have it. As a gift."

"That's very generous, but I want to pay for it. Would £300 cover it?"

"Three hundred?" Marcie gulped back her surprise. "Um, okay. That's good." It would sure help her budget. She could buy a new cell phone.

Greg pulled a wallet from his back pocket, the movement making his T-shirt stretch more tightly across his chest. Marcie had taken sculpture classes in college. Greg would make a great sculptor's model. Preferably nude.

"What?" She'd totally missed what he'd said as he pulled three notes from his wallet and handed them to her.

"I should take this directly to the framer before something happens to it." He looked up at the thickening clouds. "Thanks, Marcie. I know my friends will treasure it." He held out his hand and she took it. It was the same firm and warm grip she remembered from that morning, like entering the warmth of home after a walk on a cold, windy day. She felt that stunning connection again. He looked at her for a long moment, as though he'd felt it, too. Then, with a word to Bobby, he walked away. Marcie curled her fingers to hold on to the warmth as she watched him go. He still limped.

When he was out of sight she sighed and looked down at her artwork. Ten done, fifty to go. She was right on schedule.

***

Greg walked away from Marcie, regret edging away the excitement he'd felt earlier. Learning she had a contract with Caledon and Bishops put a spanner in the works. He couldn't wait five weeks until she finished her current project. Old Gregor had given him four weeks to prove he could come up with a worthwhile idea. Besides, Caledon and Bishops would likely have her signed to a new contract before then. And he didn't doubt Fairmont would have a licensing agreement for her, too. It was a good company, and strong competition. His grandfather had been grousing about taking it over someday.

Greg considered his options as he walked to the framer's shop and left the watercolor, plus an incentive to expedite the job. His best hope to acquire rights to Marcie's artwork and to sign her to a licensing contract would be to offer her a better deal, make her want to switch to McInnis House Press. To do that he'd have to keep close to her. And to do that he'd have to charm her. He was surprisingly uncomfortable with that idea. Not because he didn't like Marcie, just the opposite. He'd enjoyed spending time with her, answering her questions about Scotland, just sitting and watching her work. But he'd lost his edge in charming the ladies after he'd lost Emma.

Marcie had a true talent and he had no doubt that in the not too distant future, she'd be well known. He'd like to help her achieve that.

He walked around the block considering his options, finally deciding that for now, keeping close would have to do.

He stopped, leaned against the sun-warmed stone of a fish and chips shop, pulled out his phone and rearranged his obligations for the weekend.

***

Across the park Marcie found a place to sit on the grass sheltered from the wind but still in the sun. Chewing her thumbnail, she sat deep in thought as she studied her next subject. She'd been sketching for almost an hour when the savory aroma of fish and chips caught her attention. Then something cold and wet touched her arm, making her jump, and she looked around to see Bobby at her elbow and Greg towering behind her. Her mouth stretched into a big grin. He did that to her. Made her feel happy for no other reason than just being there.

"Hungry?" He crouched beside her, then sat on the grass. "Finish your sketch, then we'll eat."

"It smells delicious. I *am* hungry, thanks." She added the last details to her vignette, then put her things away.

"You always work from that wee pallet?"

"Only when I travel."

"What other equipment do you carry?"

"This is my water container." She held out a plastic camping flask and showed him how the little metal cup served as a miniature rinse bucket. Since he seemed sincerely interested, she opened her zippered pencil bag and showed him its contents. "Brushes, mechanical pencils, extra leads, erasers, a sharpener, a small ruler."

"I've seen artists with easels, chairs and huge tackle boxes."

"I travel light."

"I guess so!" He opened the paper-wrapped fish and chips and laid it on the grass between them, then handed her some paper napkins and a bottle of sparkling water.

Greg gave Bobby a chip, then reminded him to stay put. Lying on his belly, wiggling with anticipation, the little dog swallowed the fried potato in one gulp. Bobby watched his master, and Marcie noticed whenever Greg looked away, the little dog inched closer.

The fresh fried cod was hot, flaky and heavenly, and Marcie was glad to see Greg had brought plenty. "I think he's jealous," she said. Bobby looked from her to Greg with the most pitiful don't-I-get-any-more look—little bushy eyebrows up, head cocked to one side, brown eyes so sad. "Can I give him a little piece?"

"Aye, but at your own risk."

"Does he bite?" Marcie hesitated.

"*Och*, no. He'll become a beggar, a leech, a wee thief."

Marcie laughed and held out a small morsel to the terrier. Bobby vacuumed it from her fingers, then moved to sit closer to her.

"I think you've won his heart."

Hmm, could the fastest way to a man's heart be not through his stomach, but through his dog's stomach? Marcie laughed at the thought.

Marcie asked Greg to suggest some locations where she might paint.

"You've been to Glencoe?" he asked.

"Yes, day before yesterday."

"Loch Leven?"

"No. Would it be worth it?"

"I think you'd like it. The turnoff to Ballachulish is on the road to Glencoe. Near the end of the loch there's a good view over the water. The light is best mid morning, it will be over your left shoulder."

Marci widened her eyes in surprise. He talked her language.

"I do a little photography," he said, "so I'm familiar with the light in the Highlands."

"I bet you never run out of opportunities for great photographs. I planned to paint the canal locks at Neptune's Staircase tomorrow morning, but if the light is good at Loch Leven, I'll go there instead. Thanks for the suggestion." She pulled out her map and he pointed out other places she might like to paint: Glenfinnan at Loch Shiel, the Well of the Seven Heads, and a place where the canal crossed over the river.

Marcie had one more thing she wanted to ask him. "The longest day of the year is in four weeks. Where's a good place to watch the midnight sun set?"

"The Arctic Circle," he said with no expression except a mischievous twinkle in his eye.

"No, I mean in Scotland. Doesn't the sun set very late on June twenty-first?"

"Aye, on the Orkneys the sun sets after ten and comes back up around three in the morning. It skims just below the horizon and seems not to set at all. It gets dim but not dark. We call it the skimmer dim."

"The skimmer dim," Marcie said wistfully, loving being in Scotland. "What about locally? Somewhere around here, but away from the city."

"There are several good overlooks in the mountains. But I wouldn't recommend going into the mountains if you're not familiar with the area. Perhaps you'd enjoy the midsummer celebrations that take place around Loch Ness."

"I'm thinking some place quieter. Reflective." She'd feel safe with him if he took her to one of those mountain overlooks.

"How long will you be in Fort William?" he asked, motioning her to take the last piece of fish.

"Another day, then I move to Fort Augustus."

"The housewarming I mentioned is this evening. Would you like to come? I know my friends would enjoy meeting the artist who painted their cottage."

Marcie looked away to hide her disappointment. *To meet the artist*, not *to meet you*. But what did she have to whine about? The most handsome man she'd ever met had just invited her out for the evening to meet his friends. She turned back to him with a smile. "I'd love to, thanks."

"Since they're close to your bed and breakfast, I'll meet you there and we'll walk. About sevenish? There'll be cocktails and tidbits."

"Yes. Seven is good." It would give her plenty of time to dress. Or maybe she should say, impress. She pulled another card from her bag and handed it to him. "This is the bed and breakfast where I'm staying. It's only four or five houses from your friends' cottage."

Greg pocketed the card and looked at his watch, gave Bobby a leftover scrap, then crumpled the papers in his large hands. He stood, once again towering above her. "See you at seven, Marcie."

"Thanks for dinner." He didn't offer his hand this time.

He turned, shot the wadded papers into a bin and sauntered off with Bobby close beside him.

Marcie watched his broad back as he crossed the green. He still limped. Her camera couldn't have done that much damage. She should have asked if his limp was from that morning. How thoughtless. His attention had carried her away and she hadn't thought of his well-being.

As Marcie watched, he reached the far side of the park, picked up the little dog, tucked it under his arm, then disappeared into a side street. She sighed, gathered her materials and returned to her bed and breakfast in the opposite direction.

***

The next morning, after negotiating the roundabout in town, Marcie found it was an easy drive to Loch Leven. The level road followed Loch Linnhe's shore, running between the smoky-blue estuary and the verdant Highland mountains. Ultramarine water, cerulean sky and a thousand different greens surrounded her. The greens reminded her of Greg's eyes, how they changed with his emotions. She'd noticed it the first few minutes they'd met. Learning his moods could take a lifetime. So far, with herself, his dog and his friends, she'd seen concern, pain, mischievousness, compassion, and affection. She could describe his eyes with the colors of the paints she knew so well. His eyes had shimmered with *viridian* green lights when he'd picked her up for the housewarming, then a subdued *chromium*-green flash of pain when they arrived at his friends' cottage. He'd seemed sincerely happy for Iona and Archie, so the pain came from another source. It had been fleeting, only when all the attention had been on her, when he'd thought no one was looking at him. But she'd seen it, just like the first time they'd met. But when she'd caught his eye, the pain vanished and he'd smiled, and her heart wobbled knowing that somehow she had alleviated his pain, if only for a few moments.

If she were lucky, they would have some time to get to know each other before she had to leave Scotland. Leaving was a thought that was getting harder to face the further she ventured into the Highlands.

She turned on to the road to Loch Leven. Heavy clouds piled up in the West in a holding pattern, waiting for the sun to warm the land so they could start their mad dash to the East to cool it off again.

The Ardgour Mountains had already lost color under the rolling gray clouds. Closer summits rose steeply, their greenery lush, their jagged black-rock tops poking at the bright blue sky.

Marcie found the place where she would paint. It was on a spit of land near the loch's end, where the road was elevated several feet above the water. It had a wide turnout and a perfect view. Ridge after ridge of the surrounding mountains dipped their toes into the water. Their greens turned to blues, then purples and grays, as they marched into the distance. Low clouds caressed distant peaks. A small tree-covered island, not far offshore, added interest.

This was what Marcie loved, being outdoors among the mountains.

With a folded beach towel as a cushion, Marcie sat on the gravel, pulled out her supplies and studied the view. As she sketched, the clouds rolled in closer, casting shadows across the scene. Mists fingered down crevasses and filled ravines. Gulls fought the wind in their attempt to argue with Mother Nature.

Lost in her craft she remembered her "date" with Greg the night before. After the first introductions to the owners of the cottage, he'd taken her around to meet the other guests. Sometimes he had wandered off to visit with someone but he'd never left her for long. He'd given her a personal tour of the cottage, explaining all that his friends' were doing to renovate it. She'd especially enjoyed their tour of the back garden in the twilight and their walk home to her bed and breakfast. His farewell had been warm and had held the promise of meeting again.

***

An hour later, as Marcie put the final touches on her painting, a car pulled up behind her. A door opened and shut. She didn't look back; she wanted to finish before the clouds won their battle with the sun. Feet crunching gravel warned her someone approached. Then she felt him behind her, watching.

"Hello, Greg," she said without turning. "Come to see if I took your advice?"

"How'd you know it was me?" He sat down next to her, a seriously professional camera slung across his broad chest, Bobby in his arms.

"I just did." She scratched Bobby under the chin, then looked up into Greg's eyes. He looked concerned. "You suggested this place, and you wanted to see my landscapes." He looked so good with his wind-ruffled hair. A long-sleeved, dark blue T-shirt stretched across his muscled back as he leaned forward to put Bobby down to wander off and sniff the shrubs, pee on the rocks and take a drink from the loch. "Am I right?" she asked.

"Partly. I do want to see your landscapes, especially this scene; it's one of my favorites. But I also regretted suggesting it when I remembered how isolated it is. I wanted to be sure you're all right."

"How chivalrous you are. I'm not afraid to sit alone, particularly in a place like this. I'd be more nervous sitting alone in the middle of some Glasgow neighborhoods." Her racing heart was almost making her breathless.

He reached for his camera. "May I shoot you while you paint?"

That was a first. People often asked her if they could watch, but no one had ever wanted to photograph her. The wind whipped her hair, making her time in front of the mirror that morning wasted effort. She reached up to refasten a barrette.

"Don't. I mean, don't be conscious of the camera. I like how the wind plays with your hair. Just be you, ignore me."

Hardly. She could never ignore him. He was too... too everything. She returned to her work, conscious of him standing, moving, crouching, coming in close. The camera's electronic noises were easier to ignore than he was. Her cheeks burned. He made her smile. He made her self-conscious. He made her aware. Done with the painting, she handed it to him. He sat next to her and compared it to the scene before him. "Superbly executed. Your colors and values are perfect."

He returned the painting and she stowed it in her bag with care.

He stood and held out a hand to her. "There's a pub at Kinlochleven. Follow me, I'll buy you a drink."

"Okay." She let him help her up, any excuse to feel his strong but gentle grip that warmed her to her toes.

As she put her bag in the car, the wind flung her hair across her face. She tucked it behind her ear and looked out over the loch again. Dark waters rippled, forming miniature whitecaps. "This is a beautiful spot. I will always remember it. So quiet, so wild and untouched."

"Aye. But not untouched, just not overdeveloped."

When Marcie turned to look at Greg, he was photographing her again. She made a silly face and slid into her car. He climbed into a white, mud-splattered Land Rover and she followed him to Kinlochleven, a little beyond the end of the loch.

They parked off the main street and walked to the pub. Weathered, wooden picnic tables with red and white-striped umbrellas flapping in the breeze lined the pavement out front. Greg had put on a lightweight jacket against the wind, his camera over one shoulder. He probably took it with him wherever he went, the way she always kept a sketchbook with her.

Marcie wore a sweater and a raincoat and was still cold. The temperature seemed to drop one degree with each cloud that scuttled over their heads. She sat with Bobby at her feet and people-watched while Greg went into the pub. Walkers and hikers ambled the streets with packs on their backs. A light drizzle started and was carried under the umbrella on the wind. A quiver of excitement tickled Marcie as she anticipated time with Greg in this quaint Scottish village. She hugged herself.

He returned with two glasses filled with amber liquid topped by a half inch of foam. "You cold?"

"No, not at all," she lied.

"I thought I saw you shiver. We can go inside."

"No, it's nice here. I like to watch the people." She took a sip.

"This'll warm you. It's locally brewed. Do you like it?"

"It's good. A bit stronger than I've had before, but good flavor." She looked under the table where Bobby lay on his master's feet. "He's sure a quiet little dog. Or exceedingly well behaved. He hasn't barked once at the strangers."

"His previous owners had him clipped."

"Clipped?"

"They had his larynx clipped. He has no voice," he said.

"Oh no. Poor thing. He can't be a watch dog."

"He lets me know if he's suspicious or alarmed." Greg reached down and caressed Bobby's ear, then sat up, both arms on the table. "Would you like to go for a walk? There's a foot path from here to Gray Mare Falls. It takes half an hour there and back."

"I'd like that." The day was getting better and better.

When they finished their beer, Greg put Bobby on a leash. The little dog skipped between them as Greg and Marcie walked in a feather-light sprinkle through the small village. Across the River Leven they turned toward the mountain that hugged the glen's north side.

"For a hundred years aluminum smelting supported this area. When the plant closed, the town reinvented itself. Now it caters to outdoor tourism."

Marcie looked up at Greg as he told her the area's history. A stray sunbeam refracted in the water droplets clinging to his damp, curling hair. His eyes changed from chromium green to olive green as the clouds opened further. She studied his face, more interested in the line of his jaw, the arch of his lips, and the texture of his skin in the sunbeam than in what he said. Studying people's faces was her job as an artist, wasn't it?

"There's a rainbow." He pointed behind her, then raised his camera.

She turned to look but the clouds closed again and it was gone. The bright spot of her trip would likely be gone, too. Greg would probably be going back to his home in Inverness soon and she would be moving on to Fort Augustus and Loch Ness. Alone.

Alone hadn't bothered her much before, but now *alone* sounded so… lonely.

So much for hoping there would be time to get to know each other.

They weren't the only ones on the trail to the waterfall. A family with three small children stopped to examine some plants. An elderly couple bickered as they strolled the path. Two teenagers scampered off and on the trail, disappearing into the gorge ahead. Greg picked Bobby up as the little dog strained to take off after the teens to join in their fun.

"This is beautiful," Marcie said when they stopped at a viewpoint. The scenery excited her and she took several snapshots, which she could paint from back home in her studio where she'd finish a few of the more detailed paintings. Of course she didn't actually have a home or a studio since her breakup with Joel. But she wouldn't think about that now.

She looked up at Greg and smiled. "I'm glad you suggested this."

They followed wooden steps down the fern-blanketed hillside, crossed a wooden bridge, then followed a path to the foot of the waterfall in a narrow canyon. Bobby squirmed in Greg's arms and he let the little dog down to explore.

Water tumbled from a crevasse above their heads. Gray rock turned black from the waterfall's spray. Green lichens thrived in the dampness, mottling the rocks with fantastic patterns. The falls flared at the base, resembling a wind-blown mare's tail. Bits of rainbow, stolen from the intermittent sun, danced in the waterfall's spray. The water rushed over rocks and tree roots on its way to join the river. Beech and yew trees grew above the ferns. Marcie took a deep breath, memorizing the herbaceous fragrances as mist from the waterfall fell softly on her face.

After several minutes, they headed back the way they had come. Just below the steps that would take them to Kinlochleven, where the path narrowed, a racket of stomping feet and youthful whoops surprised them. Greg pulled Marcie effortlessly off the path with an arm around her waist. They lost their balance on the rocky dirt and Marcie landed against his chest as several teen-agers raced down the steps and past them to the waterfall. Alarmed, but feeling safe within Greg's arms, Marcie didn't move. She liked leaning into him. She felt his warmth spread through her as if she were standing next to a campfire. It took all her will power not to wrap her arms around him and lay her head on his shoulder. Would she ever get another chance to be so close? When she looked up she found him studying her, his gaze a caress. When his eyes dropped to her mouth, her heart rose to her throat. She thought he might kiss her. How astonishing would that be?

Then she *was* astonished as he lowered his head and his lips touched hers in a soft, warm exploration; brief, but memorable, making her incapable of movement except to lift her head and do a little exploring of her own. Then she did wrap her arms around him and felt his circle her.

Bobby tugging at his leash brought them both back to their surroundings. Greg touched a forefinger to her lips and smiled. And she learned another of his emotions: desire. She took a deep breath, unwound herself from him and stepped back to the path. He took her hand and they climbed the steps. It was a cliché, she knew, but Marcie felt as if she floated up those steps.

"Let's explore the village," Greg said. "Then we'll have something to eat."

"Okay." She wasn't cold anymore.

***

Greg had almost pushed Marcie away from him after pulling her from the path. Having her so close had been like a physical blow, a reminder of what he'd lost. The strength of it had nearly taken his breath. Then the past had melted as her warmth seeped into his cold heart and he couldn't resist kissing her sensuous mouth. He needed to stay close, but not that close. It wasn't a good idea to become too involved, to lead her to expect more than he could give.

He'd wanted something new and fresh to concentrate on, to help him forget that his father was gone, or how he'd failed Emma and his friends. What a sick joke fate had played on him in that what he had found to help him forget the past also reminded him of the past.

But he needed Marcie's art to complete his plans for the new line. Alienating her now would risk everything: the new line, the licensing plans, his place in the family business.

Pain pierced Greg's foot as they climbed the steps to Kinlochleven. He welcomed it; it took his mind off what he couldn't change. Maybe he should find another source for something new and fresh. But he wanted Marcie's art; it fit his plans so perfectly. The fact that she was already signed with another publisher was going to make achieving his goal that much harder. Well, he needed a challenge, a purpose. He welcomed it.

"What's that conical peak called?" Marcie pointed to the highest peak in the direction of Loch Leven.

"Sgorr na Ciche or the Pap of Glencoe. Glencoe is on the other side. There's a footpath to the top, five miles or so. Perhaps someday you'll walk it."

"I'd like to, if you'll show me the way. The views would be worth it. Have you been to the top?"

"Several times. And yes, the views are worth it, but not much to see on a day like this."

The rain stopped when they reached the pub and the wind relaxed into a breeze. Greg left Marcie at the table outside with Bobby, a damp fluff ball on her lap, while he stepped into the pub to order lunch. Outside again, he placed a tray on the table and sat.

"What's that?"

"Scotch eggs."

"I've never seen one." She leaned closer to look as he took one and cut it in half.

"A boiled egg covered with sausage, breaded and deep fried. Maybe not healthy food but filling, warm and delicious. Pub food." *Comfort food.*

"Um, tasty," she said around a mouthful.

He laughed. He hadn't found much to laugh about in a long time. Marcie was helping him find laughter again. "I'm glad you like it." He liked her enthusiasm and her interest in everything around her. He'd noticed it the first day they'd met, as she seemed to look at the world in wonder. At Iona and Archie's housewarming last night she'd been the center of attention as the other guests praised her talent; yet she was just as interested in each person she met and managed to connect with them all in a quiet, unassuming way. She'd looked bright and young and beautiful in a pretty sundress when he'd picked her up at the bed and breakfast.

He had to admit, the more time he spent with Marcie the more interested he was in her outside of her artwork. That just made the whole package more attractive.

"I notice you're still limping," she said, surprising him.

"I'm so sorry I hurt you with my camera."

"You didn't. My limp is from a couple years ago." It was all the explanation he gave. He couldn't talk about it. It was hard enough to live with the memories; he wasn't going to encourage the pain by saying more.

"I'm glad I didn't cause it, but I'm sorry you still have pain."

"It's not much. I appreciate your concern, but you needn't worry about it."

She smiled, which just irritated him. She should have been mad or hurt, the way he'd dismissed her concern so coldly.

"I brought more watercolors to show you, the ones I did between Oban and Fort William, the Sea Life Centre at Loch Creran, Castle Stalker, Port Appin. They're in the car. "

"Excellent. I want to see them."

By the time they finished their meal and returned to their cars it had started to sprinkle again. Marcie invited Greg to sit in her car to look at the paintings.

The car became a small and intimate space when he folded himself into the passenger seat. She handed him several small paintings and he looked at each one, half his mind on her incredible artwork, half on her. She sat with Bobby on her lap, cuddling the terrier as if he were her own pet.

"Perfect. Brilliant. You have a special talent, Marcie. I like how you captured the rain clouds in this one."

"Thanks." She smiled. He loved her smile, so freely given. "I'm really getting excited about the finished book. It will be a big boost to my career plans. I need a good body of work like this to show agents. Not just what I produced in college, but real world stuff, work that shows I'm consistent and productive."

"This is certainly a good start." He didn't need to see any more to be convinced. He flipped through the stiff watercolor papers again, feeling the excitement of discovery. "Brilliant fishing boats. Detailed but not fussy. Vivid, fresh." He turned in the seat to better face her. "I'd like you to work for us, Marcie. I can offer you a multi-book contract and a lucrative licensing agreement. The first book would be the west coast, Oban and the near Hebrides. The second would be Fort William and the Lochabr area, the third Loch Ness, Inverness and the east coast."

She looked excited, then concerned. "As I explained yesterday, I'm already contracted to do pretty much the same area for Caledon and Bishops. I appreciate the offer. Perhaps we can talk again after this job is done, in about five weeks."

That was too long for Greg's plans. Even without considering his four-week deadline, he wanted to get his proposal in and agreed to soon so the first book could be included on the list they were compiling now. So his grandfather would have no more reasons to doubt Greg's ability to run the Inverness office. "I can offer you more. I've mentored young artists—photographers— before. I can help you with licensing agreements to include products besides those in the McInnis House Press line."

"That's very generous. But I'm happy with what I have. I don't want to jeopardize my relationship with Caledon and Bishops. I have your number, I'll call when the job is finished." She held out her hands for the paintings. As he handed them over, Bobby scrambled onto his lap and licked his chin.

Greg could see he'd offended Marcie. She'd definitely cooled toward him. But if he had to wait much longer to sign her, he'd lose his window of opportunity with his grandfather. "You're moving on to Fort Augustus next?"

"Tonight's my last night in Fort William. Tomorrow I'll be painting around Gairlochy and Loch Lochy, as you suggested. I'll stay in Fort Augustus for a few days."

"You'll like Fort Augustus. It's a pretty town, quaint and charming. The canal runs through town center and the locks attract tourists. There are beautiful flower displays lockside." He pulled the university card she'd given him the day before from his wallet . "Which number should I use to contact you?"

"I dropped my cell phone in a… a public toilet. Blame it on jet lag. The e-mail address is good. I try to check it every day."

Without a phone he wasn't sure how he'd find her in the crowded little town, but he'd try. At least he could leave her an e-mail message. He so desperately needed her artwork he'd do whatever he had to do. But for now he could tell she wanted him to leave.

"Thanks for an enjoyable day, Marcie." He really had enjoyed it and hoped he hadn't ruined his chances with her.

"Thanks for lunch. And for showing me the falls. I think I'll go back and do a painting. The rain has stopped."

He left her then, wanting to kiss her, but knowing to do so would push it. Keeping track of her, as he worked out a way to win her over from Caledon and Bishops before it was too late was enough for now.

***

Driving back to Fort William, Greg thought of his time with Marcie. He'd enjoyed photographing her as she worked, capturing her intensity, zooming in when she became self-conscious, her cheeks rosy. She was so vital, so alive.

For the first time in years he wanted to be outside, having an adventure. He wanted to show Marcie all his favorite places in the Highlands. He knew she would appreciate the beauty.

It was going to be hard to keep their relationship professional when he wanted to know her personally. Could he be approaching the other end of that long, black tunnel of grief? Maybe.

Was he ready? He was ready to find out.

Loch Leven and the Pap of Glen Coe

CHAPTER THREE

After Greg had driven out of sight Marcie pounded her fists on the steering wheel. She'd known him two days and already he was turning out to be like all the other men she'd known, sending mixed signals, always having an agenda.

Why'd he kiss me if he's only interested in my art?

He'd offered to mentor her. Well, she'd been a protégée before and it hadn't worked out so well. She was past that stage anyway. She was on her own, responsible for her own career, ready and willing to meet all challenges.

She repacked her painting bag with fresh paper and the supplies she'd need and got out of the car. It took her half the time to reach the falls as it had with Greg. With him she'd wanted to make the walk last and had dawdled at every scenic opportunity.

She found a spot away from the waterfall's spray and soothed herself by getting lost in the act of creation. By the time she had completed the watercolor painting, she was calm. After that she did a couple of small botanical vignettes, and a sketch of a child crouched before the stream, enthralled with floating, swirling twigs he'd dropped into an eddy. His parents stood close by, allowing him to explore and get dirty while being sure he was safe. Seeing this reinforced Marcie's desire to have a family of her own. She wanted to share the beauty of nature with her kids. She wanted them to be free to explore and at the same time to feel safe in a family where love and support were top priority. It was what she'd longed for as a child without being able to verbalize it. This opportunity could lay the foundation for the realization of that dream. She wanted her family to be whole, with a man who was a loving husband and a good daddy to their kids. But if that didn't happen, she'd build her own family. As an illustrator with a good licensing agreement, she'd be able to make her own work schedule and she'd earn a good wage. She could adopt or use a sperm service. She'd grown up alone, she could start her family alone. Then she'd never be alone again.

***

Sunday morning Greg left his townhouse in Inverness for a run and lifted his face to the breeze as if it could blow away remnants of the recurring nightmare that had disturbed his night. He'd thought it had stopped, but the Himalaya book with its reminders of that disaster must have triggered its return.

The early summer sun tinged the clouds pink. Screeching gulls overhead made him feel at home. Everything looked crisp and fresh. He loved living in Inverness. He loved living. He'd come too close to dying on Mt. Everest not to appreciate his life. His father hadn't made it home three years ago and Emma hadn't made it home a year later when Greg had tried to recapture his father's dream. He was grateful for what he had. And finally he was beginning to enjoy life again.

Greg slowed as he turned for home. Going uphill still caused trouble with his injured foot. He could tolerate the pain; it was the lack of balance that was so hard to adjust to.

After a shower and dressing for work, he pulled out his phone and looked for a message from Marcie. He found a short email.

Greg,
I'll be painting at Loch Sheil today.
I'm sure it's out of your way so don't think
you need to look after me. I'll be fine.
MW

Brr! A bit of frost there. He shouldn't have tried to recruit her when she was perfectly happy with her situation. He couldn't afford to alienate her. He needed to back pedal.

Marcie,
Enjoy the loch, it's a beautiful
location. The aqueduct is impressive. Be sure
to climb to the top of the Prince Charlie
monument. Great views.
Greg

He also couldn't afford to lose track of her. With the right guidance, the right mentoring, Marcie could negotiate more than one lucrative licensing contract. Tomorrow he'd email her and make an appointment to meet. An appointment, not a date. This was business. He could mentor her, but that was all. He'd gone too far at Gray Mare Falls. In a weak moment he'd crossed the line and put his plans in jeopardy. He couldn't take that risk again. He needed to keep his mind on task or he'd lose his place in the family business.

***

Monday morning, Greg entered his office and sighed when he saw the pile of mail and messages sitting in his inbox. He'd been dumped into the deep end of this job, taking over for his father. But he was a fast learner and his father had been training him since he'd left university. Since he'd been a boy, actually. He just hadn't put all his attention to the training because he'd never thought he would be called to take over so soon. Almost overnight he'd gone from working as lead photographer for the family business, with the freedom to travel and work at his own schedule, to CEO of the Inverness branch. Now his grandfather was pulling back. Calling him an *interim* CEO. Old Gregor's ultimatum hung over Greg like a storm cloud.

Before looking through his mail from the last few days, Greg sat, booted up his computer, and emailed Marcie.

49

```
Hello Marcie,
    Where will you'll be painting next?
I'll find you and if you need suggestions for
places to paint in that area, I'll be glad to
help out. Maybe we can fit in another walk.
    Greg
```

He sent the email, then picked up his mail and messages.

"Good morning, Greg. Glad you're back. Coffee?" Judy Fraser had been his father's assistant and now was his. She'd helped him make the transition from capricious photographer to reliable chief executive officer. *Interim chief executive officer.* He owed Judy more than he could ever repay.

"Aye."

She brought the coffee on a tray with two buttered scones, and stood before him, tall and neat and nice to look at. She had curly red hair pinned up in an artless style that suited her. She needed little makeup and her skirted suit was exactly right. "Join me?" he asked.

"Sorry, I've got that report on tourism from the Far East. It's making me daft, but it should be done in time for the meeting Thursday. You've only three meetings today. Pratt canceled."

"Good. Seems like I never have time to catch up on what I didn't have time to do in the first place."

"I hear you there," Judy agreed. "Were the meetings in Fort Will tough? You look a wee bit nackered."

Greg sat back. Judy could read him like a book. "It was a tough weekend in some ways, but the meetings went well. Granddad found out about the book. It was a little rough. He wasn't well pleased. And the reminders..." He knew she'd understand what he meant without explaining more.

"I'm sorry. Reminders will hit you when you least expect them and are least prepared. They'll knock you back into the black hole if you're not careful. Is that what happened?"

"Aye. Took me to the edge, but I didn't fall in. Each time it gets a little easier not to fall in."

"They say it will get better with time, though sometimes it doesn't seem so, does it?" she said with understanding. She'd lost her husband shortly before his father had died. It was a double blow to her as his father had been well liked and revered by his employees.

"That day seems a long way off." He knew she was talking about the loss of his father and the trouble his team had faced on the mountain. He'd never told her about his feelings for Emma, or that they'd been married by a passing American preacher of dubious qualification in Nepal, that the marriage probably hadn't been legal. They'd felt married. "The weekend wasn't all bad. I met a woman—"

"You met someone?" Judy sat in one of the chairs in front of his desk and leaned forward. "What's she like?"

"Don't get ahead of yourself. I was going to say that I met a woman artist whose work fits the new guide book project exactly. Unfortunately, she's contracted to someone else and won't be finished with them until the end of June."

"Then she'll be free to work with us?"

"Not exactly. She returns to the States then. She's from San Francisco. That's a problem because Granddad gave me an ultimatum this weekend. I need to give a killer presentation on my idea or he'll bring in Uncle Rowan to do my job."

Judy sagged back in her chair. "That's harsh. Because of the Himalaya trip?"

"Aye. I am now *interim* CEO."

"He didn't. He demoted you? Old coot."

"And, the artist is presently contracted to Caledon and Bishops."

"No way. Did you tell her about the hostile takeover?"

"No. You know Granddad would disinherit me if he knew I spoke of it to anyone outside the company. Besides, it's all talk." Greg and Judy had jokingly dubbed his grandfather's plan as *the hostile takeover*.

"You should tell her, she has a right to know that her contract is in jeopardy."

"You think it's gone that far?"

"Didn't you know? There have been negotiation meetings for a month, now. I thought you knew."

"No. Am I so insignificant around here that my assistant is more informed than I am? He was telling me I wasn't mature enough for this job. How mature is he, playing petty games? Tell me what you know."

"Not much. Mostly rumors, really. Even so, if the buyout doesn't happen in the next month, before this woman finishes her jog, her project could become a casualty of the war, so to speak. I think you should warn her. She's probably spending a lot of money and time on something that might not happen. Then you can sign her."

"I can't promise her anything until Granddad gives me the okay. He won't give me the okay until I give him a brilliant presentation, and I can't give him a presentation without her artwork and she won't lend artwork that she sees as belonging to Caledon and Bishops, our competitor."

"*Och*, you're making it so complicated. Tell her and let her deal with it." Judy stood. "I've got to get on that tourism report." She returned to her desk in the outer office.

Greg was considering Judy's argument when his phone pinged. He was glad to see a text from Marcie.

> Hi Greg. Got a new phone. I'm going 2
> Spean Bridge and Loch Laggan this morn. Per
> UR suggestion. MW

The text lacked her usual warmth, and he was pretty sure that was intentional. He hadn't handled their last conversation well. He'd upset her.

Greg checked his calendar, made a few calls. His day looked flexible between nine and noon. He had a lunch meeting at half noon, so that gave him three hours he could take to find Marcie, do some damage control. Her artwork was the key to his success. Finding her and apologizing was important enough to leave the office for a few hours. But he hadn't decided yet what he would tell her about Caledon and Bishops.

He was so burned, or if he admitted it, hurt, that his grandfather hadn't included him in his plans to court Caledon and Bishops. He could just hear Uncle Rowan snickering at Greg's exclusion. He needed to take his mind off that.

At ten past nine, he told Judy he'd be available on his mobile and took off to find Marcie at Spean Bridge.

After stopping at his townhouse to change and gather Bobby, he lost a little of his usual patience with the tourist traffic—after all, tourists constituted a large part of his family's customer base. Soon he left the town traffic behind and was driving the road alongside Loch Ness. He knew the road well and relaxed, enjoying the view.

An hour later, he turned onto the road to Spean Bridge. He'd see Marcie again and they could walk by the loch, stop for...

Greg's thoughts were interrupted as three cars ahead of him, he saw a plum of dust rise and moments later hearing the squeal of breaks and crunch of metal. His first reaction was to curse the delay it was likely to cause him. He couldn't see the vehicles involved. The car directly behind the crash went around and sped off. The car in front of Greg stopped suddenly. Greg, already applying his breaks, pulled onto the verge beside it and stopped. A man jumped out of the car and ran to the middle of the road pulling out a phone. Greg ran toward the wreck. The cars were at an angle in the left lane—one going, one coming, their driver sides smashed against each other.

As the dust cleared Greg saw a small blue car and... his breath caught... a green Rover.

Marcie?

***

Greg ran the remaining distance and pulled the passenger door open, his heart pounding in his chest. "Marcie! Are you hurt?" Both her arms were up protecting her head. The air bag lay deflated. She didn't move. "Marcie, are you all right?"

"I-I'm okay. Okay. I..." She lowered her arms and looked at him, her eyes wide with shock. "Greg?"

"I'm here." He could see blood on the right side of her forehead. The side impact must have thrown her into the driver door window. "Let me check you." He carefully felt the back of her neck, her arms, legs. "Can you breathe deeply?"

She tried, then winced. "No. It hurts. But I'm okay. Just give me a minute." She might have broken or bruised her ribs. "What're you doing here?"

"I came to see you. Did you get my text?" he asked while checking for other injuries.

"No. This isn't good, is it?"

"Shush. Don't talk. Don't move."

Then Greg smelled petrol. He needed to get Marcie out of the car. "I'm going to slide you over the seat, Marcie. I'll try not to hurt you, but we need to get you out of here." He put one arm under her knees and one behind her shoulders, lifting and pulling as he backed out. Then he carried her away from the wreck. He set her on her feet but quickly scooped her up again when he saw her legs give way.

"I'm o-okay. I just need a minute to c-catch my breath."

Greg sat on a stone wall away from the wreck and held her on his lap. She was having difficulty breathing, definitely a sign of damaged ribs.

The other driver was standing on the side of the road holding a cloth to his head, the driver who had called in the wreck supporting him. He seemed steady, not intoxicated. Looking at the cars Greg could tell the driver of the blue car had come at Marcie head-on, in the wrong lane. Both had swerved at the last moment, colliding the driver sides. Both cars were totaled.

Sirens sounded in the distance. The relief of hearing them did little to assuage his guilt. Marcie had been on her way to a venue he'd suggested. If she'd stayed in Fort Augustus, as she had originally planned, she would be happily painting right now, not in pain with every breath.

He brushed away the chill of a cold sweat from his forehead. The conditions were vastly different, but two years ago he'd held another woman in his arms. Only she had lost her struggle to breathe. He'd take care of Marcie, make sure she received the best care. Make sure she survived. He didn't think he could take losing another person he cared for.

"You're going to be all right." He wished he had a towel or a cloth to put against the cut on her forehead. Then he remembered his handkerchief, pulled it from his breast pocket and held it firmly against the wound, not wanting to hurt her, but needing to stop the blood. Her face was so pale in contrast to the dark red that streaked her face and throat, spattered over her T-shirt and onto her right arm. Her left arm was wound tightly around his neck and she rested her head against his shoulder.

"I'm so glad… you're here," she said.

"Help is coming. You'll feel better soon." He wanted to wrap his arms tightly around her, but was afraid it would cause her more pain.

***

The paramedics arrived and since Marcie had suffered more injury than the other driver, they started treating her immediately. Which meant Greg had to give her up to them. He stayed close and just as they were about to put her into the ambulance she gripped his hand.

"My things… in the car. My watercolors. My passport and credit cards… my new phone. Can you get them out?" Just then the paramedic clamped an oxygen mask over her face and all he could see was the pain in her eyes, the pleading. He wanted to go with her in the ambulance to be sure she was all right and taken care of. But he wanted to retrieve her things, Bobby was in his car and he needed to get his own car out of the way.

He called Judy to let her know what had happened and that he'd be delayed.

"Is there anything I can do?"

"Aye, call the hospital in an hour or so. See if Marcie is in Casualty or if she's in hospital. Her last name is Winters."

"Okay. One other thing. A package arrived from your grandfather just after you left. By personal messenger."

Greg sighed. He was torn between wanting to be with Marcie and keeping up with his grandfather's demands. He wanted to be sure she was okay, but if he ignored his grandfather he might not have a job.

"What's in the package?" He almost didn't want to know.

He could hear Judy tearing it open, then flipping through papers. "Looks like reports on Caledon and Bishops. Do you think the hostile takeover is happening sooner than we thought?"

"*Och*, I hope not. Not now." He pushed his hand through his hair, then groaned as he saw a policeman approach. "I have to talk to one of the officers here. I'll call you later. Look through the files and see what you can make of them. I know you're rushed with that tourism report, but if this is about the buyout, you'll have to redo your report anyway." He ended the call and turned to the officer.

After describing what little he'd witnessed, several times, Greg was allowed to take Marcie's personal belongings out of the wrecked Rover and put them in his car. He got in, turned back to Inverness and took the road more carefully than he had on his way out. Seeing that wreck was enough to make anyone drive more carefully.

***

After stopping at his townhouse to change from his stained suit to jeans and T-shirt, Greg pulled into the parking lot at the Inverness hospital, then called Judy as he walked to the entrance. "Have any info on Marcie?"

"She's in room 232. They'll only give updates of her condition to family. Old Gregor called. He wants you to look through these papers and get right back to him."

"She's from the States, just visiting. She has no one here to help her. I'll be back at the office as soon as I see that Marcie is all right. Stall Granddad if he calls."

"I hope she isn't hurt so badly that she can't paint for you."

Greg hadn't thought of that. He'd been too occupied with the emergency. But now the idea dug at him. Which was more important to him? Marcie's welfare or his agenda?

"I'm sorry," Judy continued. "I didn't mean to imply that you only cared about her artwork and not her personally."

Personally? Did he care about her personally? He'd grown fond of her. No, more than that. She was beginning to fill an empty, cold space in his heart. Her warmth, her humor, and her gumption in traveling to a foreign country to pursue her goals spoke to him on an elemental level. They both had lofty aspirations. He wanted to line them up into one seamless goal, something they could work on together for years to come. He liked the sound of that.

"I'll get back to the office as soon as I can." He ended the call and entered the hospital.

***

Marcie woke and wished she hadn't. Oblivion was preferable to the pain. She lay motionless. Even moving her head to check out her surroundings was too much.

Flashes of memory strobed across her mind's eye when she closed her eyes: the car suddenly in her path, trees spinning by, metal crunching, glass shattering, someone pulling her out. She'd dreamt it was Greg. Was it? No, he couldn't have gotten there so quickly. How would he even know about the crash? It didn't matter, in her mind it was he she'd clung to in her confusion; it was he who'd soothed her with his calm voice and comforting words.

There had been sirens and horns and a lot of jostling. People had asked her questions she couldn't answer. Bright lights. Noises she hadn't recognized.

A woman in scrubs approached. "How are you feeling, luv?"

"Like I've been tumbled in a commercial clothes dryer."

"Good, you have a sense of humor." The nurse keyed something into a handheld device.

"What hospital is this? Where?"

"Inverness."

"Do you have some aspirin or ibuprofen?"

"Oh, honey, I have something better." She took an empty IV bag off the rack beside Marcie's bed and put a full one on. "There's a wee bit of something in this that will help. Try to relax. The doctor will be by soon to check how you're doing. By the time she's done this will have taken away the pain."

christy olesen

Castle Stalker between Oban and Fort William

CHAPTER FOUR

Greg found room 232. There were four beds and Marcie was at the end near a window. When he reached her his breath stopped. Surrounded by white sheets, eyes closed, pale, so still, he feared for a moment she might be gone. Visions of another woman, white in death, motionless in the frozen wilderness, left him lightheaded.

Then Marcie breathed deeply, winced, and he was able to breathe again, able to look past her pallor and assess her injuries. The bed was elevated and light from the window slanted across her face. A large blue-and-purple bump with a few stitches colored her forehead over a black-and-blue right eye. Her right arm was bandaged from palm to elbow.

She looked so fragile, like the porcelain figurines his mother collected. He leaned against the window frame, shaken.

A nurse walked by, smiled at Greg, then checked Marcie's IV.

"Is she sedated?" he whispered.

"I just gave her a dose, but you have a few minutes before it takes effect." The nurse touched Marcie's shoulder. "You have a visitor. He can stay for a few minutes."

Marcie opened her big blue eyes; only they weren't big but squinted in pain as she looked at him. It took him a moment to realize light from the window behind him was too bright. He pulled the utilitarian curtain closed, then turned back to her. "How are you feeling?" A totally inadequate question.

"How'd you know I was here?"

"Paramedics told me."

"Were you there? I thought I was hallucinating. How did you get there so fast?"

Greg pulled a nearby chair to the side of the bed and sat. "I was just a few cars behind you. I wanted to meet you at Spean Bridge. I saw the wreck happen. Well, almost saw it."

"Was it my fault?"

"No, not at all. The other driver pulled out from a side street and forgot to stay on the left. You maneuvered brilliantly, saved yourself from a head on collision."

"I did? Is he okay? Was anyone else injured?"

"He was ambulatory, but the paramedics took him to be examined."

"What about the rental car? Will I have to pay for it?"

"Don't worry about it. The police are investigating the scene, but you were clearly not at fault. The leasing company has insurance to cover their costs. You're safe now. Concentrate on recuperating."

She closed her eyes and covered them with her hand, then winced when she touched the bruise on her temple. "God, I have such a headache... I think... I'm going to be... sick..."

Panicked, Greg stood, looked around and found an empty plastic pitcher. With an arm behind Marcie's shoulders, he lifted her.

"It's okay," she said, waving her hand in dismissal. "It's passed."

He laid her back but didn't take his hand from her shoulder for a moment. "Are you sure? I can call the sister."

"My sister's in New York. Don't look so worried, I don't get sick easily. I'm better now. I think the meds are working." She closed her eyes but he could tell she was still in pain.

"I meant the nurse, but if you need me to, I can call your sister in New York."

"No, she's too busy."

"It's no wonder you've got headache. That bump's the size of a golf ball."

"I must look awful." She opened her eyes halfway, drowsy and unfocused. "You know, I don't think I even care right now. But I'm glad you're here. I like you. It's a comfort to know I have a friend in Scotland. Do you ever wear a kilt?"

"I was wearing one the day we met." Aye, the meds were working.

"I remember, you looked great. Joel wouldn't. His knees are too knobly."

Joel?

"Do me a favor and tell Joel…I'll be…late. Remind him to bring the answers."

"Don't worry about anything. Rest. I'll take your belongings to the office until you're well enough to collect them."

"Oh, thanks… I really… appreciate…." Marcie succumbed to the sedative and closed her eyes.

Greg looked at her for a moment, the plastic pitcher dangling from his hand. He could see the tension melt from her body, the worry ease from her face, her hand unclench. He reached out to touch her hair, then pulled back before his fingers felt the silky strands.

This was his fault. He'd suggested Spean Bridge, and now… It would affect her job, if not end it.

He put the pitcher down, gently squeezed Marcie's hand, then reluctantly left her side.

At the reception desk, Greg asked about Marcie's condition and how long they expected to keep her in hospital.

"Are you family?"

"No, she has no family in Scotland. I'm her employer." Which wasn't far from the truth *if* he could sign her to McInnis House Press.

"She'll be here a day or so. She's had a shock but is not badly injured. Can we have you as a contact?" She handed him a form.

"Yes." He filled in the form and handed it back. "The bump to her head?"

"No concussion, if that's what you're asking."

"Head injuries can turn... fatal."

"That's why she's here," the nurse said with a bit of impatience. Then her voice softened. "It's just a bump. Laceration on the right forearm. Bruised ribs, small contusions as expected in an accident. We see quite a few Americans in our A&E. They forget to drive on the left."

***

Marcie woke in the night not quite remembering where she was. An eerie sulfur glow seeped through the curtains at the window so she could just see her surroundings. The gentle snores of women in nearby beds blended with the hums and clicks of hospital equipment. An acrid, antiseptic smell threatened to turn her stomach.

How could this happen? She'd planned for every contingency: lost money, lost passport, lost reservations. But never lost *everything.*

If her watercolors were lost or ruined in the wreck, an appointment with Ms. Roth would be moot, if Joel was able to get her one as he'd promised.

But Greg had come and said he had all her things. She wondered if anything had been damaged. Then she worried about the future. What would she do now? Where could she go? How long before she could travel? How would she complete her job? What would happen to her contract?

She needed answers, not questions.

Make a plan. First, she'd call Mr. Fairmont, let him know what had happened. Then contact the rental company, settle with them and get another car. If they'd let her have one.

Make a list. Follow up. It will be all right.

A couple days' rest to get over the shock, then back on schedule.

Greg had left his work to meet her at Spean Bridge. He'd pulled her from the wreck. He'd come to the hospital to be sure she was okay. Just thinking about him made her feel safe, grounded. She had a friend in Scotland. More than a friend.

I'm falling for him. What a stupid thing to do. With a little over four weeks left in Scotland she shouldn't be putting her heart in danger.

The night nurse came and gave her another sedative. "You'll feel much better in the morning," she whispered and placed a reassuring hand on Marcie's shoulder. The one that wasn't bruised.

***

Monday evaporated. Greg missed all his meetings and, in fact, had never made it back to the office. He'd ended up placing Marcie's things in his home office, then set about making calls to take care of as many things as he could to help Marcie out. He contacted the car hire company, the bed and breakfast where she'd been staying, and he'd left a message for Mr. Fairmont.

More than once he looked over at Marcie's things piled in the corner. He could easily borrow a few watercolors, have them mounted in a presentation folder, then use them to persuade his grandfather to accept his proposal. But he couldn't betray Marcie's trust. And he'd never used underhanded schemes to get his way. Well, if he didn't count not telling his grandfather about the Himalayan expedition.

***

The next morning Greg returned to his office. He sat at his desk and tried to concentrate on catching up. But his mind kept wandering to Marcie. Why did this have to happen to her?

His thoughts were interrupted by the buzzing of his intercom.

"Your grandfather's on line one. Sounds agitated," Judy said.

"He's always agitated." Greg hesitated, sighed, then picked up the phone. His *good morning* was ignored.

"I sent a courier over yesterday with some important papers for you to examine and never heard from you. It's important to keep up with and acknowledge interoffice communications. Did it arrive?"

"Yes, Granddad. I have it here in front of me."

"Why didn't you call at once to let me know you had it? I paid an exorbitant fee to have that personally couriered to you."

"Sorry, I've been out of the office until now."

"Doing what?"

Was his grandfather checking up on him, making sure he was doing his job? "I was helping someone who was in a collision."

His grandfather ignored that statement. "The packet of materials is regarding Caledon and Bishops."

"Oh, the hostile takeover." Greg said it quietly, but his grandfather had good hearing.

"Don't be belligerent!"

"Sorry, sir. I didn't know you were this far into your plan."

Again, his comment was ignored. "I want you to look them over. There's a budget, assets and liabilities, debts and creditors, and contracts. Call me first thing in the morning. And remember, not a word to anyone. If the Caledon and Bishops staff hear of it, they'll all take off. They got some good talent we want to keep. And we can't take a chance the media gets hold of the information. Understand?"

"Yes, sir. Of course." Greg wasn't sure how he'd get through the stack of papers in front of him; it would take all day. Then he realized, if his grandfather's plan to buy out Caledon and Bishops was going forward sooner than expected, it meant Marcie's contract would soon be under the McInnis House Press banner. Then it would just be a matter of Greg transferring her contract from Mr. Fairmont to Greg's office. That sounded rather unethical. He'd have to work that one out. Maybe something in the reports would help.

When Greg's grandfather had first mentioned his intention to take over Caledon and Bishops Greg could have cared less. He was struggling just to keep his branch of the business going without too many costly mistakes. So many times he'd wished he had his father to consult. But then, if his father were still alive, Greg wouldn't need to take over his father's job. He'd be off somewhere photographing exotic places for the next guide book his father planned to publish.

Greg had always loved and admired his father, but, except for the occasional groom-the-heir-to-take-over-one-day lessons, they hadn't spent much time together. Their interests and responsibilities had taken them in different directions.

This day was filled with makeup meetings and correspondence catch-up, but he found time to study the papers in between. At six Greg bundled the papers into his briefcase to take home. He'd be more comfortable in his father's old leather easy chair at home than at his desk at the office. He threw in his red copy editing pen and headed for the door.

Judy was packing up her things for the day.

"You're late tonight." She always left promptly at five-thirty.

"I wanted to finish the tourism report. With the Caledon and Bishops negotiations escalating I wanted to clear my desk. Besides, with my son gone I don't really have a reason to go home on time."

"Is Dafe enjoying his time in Wales?"

"Yes, very much. His grandfather is teaching him Welsh. He's learning his heritage."

"That's important," Greg said. He appreciated his own heritage more as he matured.

"Do you need help going over those papers? I could take part of them home, then brief you in the morning."

"You sure? I wouldn't ask, but you'd understand the stat tables better than I can. There's not many." He placed the briefcase on her desk and pulled some sheets from the packet. "Thanks. By the way, would you be willing to let Marcie stay in your spare room for a few days?"

"I don't have a spare room. It's a two bedroom cottage."

"Right." He had four guest rooms in his home, but they were all upstairs, gutted for renovation, and he was seldom home. Judy's cottage was small, cozy, all on one floor, easier to get around in for someone recovering from injuries. Moreover, Judy usually left work on time and often went home for lunch.

"Since Dafe's in Trefriw for a fortnight. I guess Marcie could use his room. If it's just for a few days."

"I'm sure she'll be ready to move on before Dafe returns."

"All right then. When can I expect her?"

christy olesen

"Tomorrow or the next day. Thanks."

***

When Greg stopped at the hospital on his way home, he walked past the gift shop, stopped and returned to it. Then, carrying a small bunch of flowers, he walked to room 232.

Marcie was sitting up in bed with a magazine open on her lap but her eyes on the view out the window. Though tear tracks streaked them, her cheeks were quite rosy, he was relieved to see. Even with her black eye she looked pretty.

An urge to protect her, to be sure she had whatever she needed tugged at his heart. He felt bad this had happened to her and he wanted to help her however he could.

He walked to the window and leaned against the frame. She didn't look at him. Then he realized she was looking at the flowers he'd forgotten in his hand. He handed them to her and was rewarded with a bright smile. "Feeling better?"

"Yes, thanks. These are beautiful. They're so fragrant, so sweet. What are they?"

"Freesia, I think."

She dabbed at her eyes with a soggy tissue. "Sorry, I'm not usually a crybaby."

"It's the shock." It was all he could think to say. He felt inadequate when what he wanted to do was make everything right for her. Her injuries would cause a setback for her. She might not be able to recover in time to complete her job. He wished he could tell her about the Caledon and Bishops buyout. Tell her she could take her time to recover and not worry about her deadline, because her contract with Caledon and Bishops would probably be cut in the transaction deal. Then he'd offer her one of his own. But nothing was certain yet and he didn't want to give her more to worry about. He wanted to tell her about his ideas, that he had a place for her when she was ready. But then again, nothing was certain and he didn't want to give her hope only to disappoint her.

She turned the flowers in her hand, studying them. Then she turned a worried face to him. "I called Caledon and Bishops but I couldn't get through to Mr. Fairmont. They wouldn't tell me where he is or when he'll be back. Just said he's temporarily unavailable."

"He's probably on a short holiday. I'm sure he'll contact you soon." He justified his lies by telling himself they would help ease Marcie's mind.

"You're right. I'm just in a panic, I guess."

"They'll discharge you tomorrow or the day after. My assistant says you can stay with her until you're ready to move on. Will that suit you?"

"Oh yes. Thanks. I wondered where I would go. You're sure she won't mind?"

"She's happy to help out. Her name is Judy Fraiser."

"How's little Bobby?"

"He's good. If you like, I can bring him by for a day to keep you company. But not just yet, when you're feeling better."

"I'd like that. I never had a dog."

By the time Greg had to leave, which came too soon, Marcie was smiling and her tears had dried up. She was an optimist, he'd learned.

"Judy will be here to pick you up when you're released."

"Thanks so much, Greg."

He left her looking at her flowers as if she'd been given the world.

He couldn't even give her the truth.

***

Greg spent the evening and well into the night reading the reports his grandfather had sent him, and wondering if Marcie was comfortable, able to sleep.

By morning he knew enough about the inner workings of Caledon and Bishops to understand his grandfather's desire to acquire the company. He knew they had a good line but he hadn't realized the extent of their diversification.

After Judy briefed him on the part of the packet she'd read, Greg called his grandfather. If his grandfather wasn't impressed with Greg's knowledge and understanding, at least he didn't make any derogatory remarks. And to Greg that was a huge relief. It gave him hope that when it came time to give his proposal, Old Gregor would listen.

***

After the euphoria of Greg's visit wore off, excitement and dread fought each other for possession of Marcie's emotions,

emotions dangerously close to the surface. She'd have to tamp them down if she was going to function once she left the hospital. The nurses expected her to be distraught and weepy, but she didn't want to bring that to Judy's home. No one would want a weepy houseguest. She laughed at herself, then wiped away another errant tear.

The freesias were gorgeous. She couldn't stop looking at them. Delicate yellow trumpets burst one after the other on gently arching stalks, and they were quite fragrant. She had a new favorite flower. Greg was so thoughtful and helpful. He must be a genuinely nice guy or he wouldn't have stopped to help her that first day. But what was his agenda? Was he truly concerned for her welfare? Or was he still wanting her talent as an artist?

All at once she realized Joel had been pushed to the back of her mind. *How fickle is that?* Joel had once been the world to her, now she'd met someone new and exciting. Yet she had dreamt of Joel during one of her naps, she remembered. Strangely, he'd been wearing a kilt and a tweed jacket. He'd walked up to her and said, "Goodbye, Marcie, and thanks for all the kisses." The dream had seemed so real. As she thought more about the dream, she realized her subconscious mind had spoken the truth. That's what their relationship had been to him, just kisses.

Good kisses. Good food. Good-bye.

Would she forget Greg so easily? Who was she kidding? She'd never forget Greg.

She might have to go home sooner than planned, and she might never see him again except for going to his office to pick up her things. That would probably be the last time.

Her soggy tissue fell apart, but it hurt too much to reach for a fresh one. Oddly though, when Greg had visited, she'd forgotten the pain, the fear, and her unknown future.

By evening Marcie felt better. More optimistic. She'd be released tomorrow and could start putting herself and her job back together.

***

The next morning the doctor visited to look at her arm. "It's coming along fine. I want you to see a physiotherapist within the week." He handed her a prescription with the therapist's name and number scrawled on it, then fitted her with a sling. "I want to caution you not to expect your hand to be as it was before the accident. It might take months of therapy to regain control."

"But I must, I'm an artist. My career depends on my being able to recover to the ability I had before this happened."

"On the side of caution, prepare yourself for not being able to paint again."

A wave of panic washed over her. *Not regain control? Not paint?* She might never be able to paint or draw again?

Despite not being one to languish in self-pity, that's exactly what Marcie allowed herself to do after the doctor's visit. So she was in tears again when a nice looking woman with pretty red hair came up to her bed.

"Oh dear. Have the waterworks sprung a leak?"

Marcie laughed and dried her eyes. "You must be Judy. Hi. I'm so grateful to you for giving me a room in your home. I can't thank you enough."

"Think nothing of it. Any friend of Greg's is a friend of mine. I brought some clothes from your duffle."

The trip from Marcie's bed to Judy's Fiat was near torture. Her chest hurt where she'd slammed into the seat belt, her ribs and hip hurt where the car door had caved in on her. Her arm and head ached. But just being outside in the fresh air was a relief. The sun shone between fast moving clouds. She breathed as deeply as she could, and found the pain had lessened. Nothing had smelled so sweet, except the freesias she still clutched in her hand, her own aromatherapy, their fragrance a link to Greg.

The little car soon pulled into a nice neighborhood of close cottages. Each with a front garden in full bloom. They stopped before a white, single-story stucco house, which glinted in the erratic sunlight. Pretty lace curtains decorated the black-framed windows. Judy parked and helped Marcie out. "There's a garage in back but I wanted to bring you in through the front door first. It makes a much nicer impression." Then she added with a little flourish, "Welcome to Fraoch Teachín."

"It's such a cute house. What does the name mean?"

"Heather Cottage." Judy opened the gate to the garden.

"What a sweet name." Once inside the small garden Marcie stopped to rest and admire the cosmos, daisies and coreopsis, and the window boxes filled with hot pink petunias cascading over their rims.

Judy unlocked the door and invited Marcie to go in before her. They stepped into a cool, narrow hall, which ran the length of the house. Rugs softened a hardwood floor and beautiful wildlife and scenic photographs hung on the walls. Judy dropped her purse and keys on a half round table in the hall below a mirror. An antique oak coat rack stood next to it with an umbrella stand filled with umbrellas and walking sticks.

"I have a small lounge here on the left. Dining room next. The kitchen beyond that. Your wee room is here on the right at the front, mine is at the back with a loo and bath between. We'll share. Feel free to use anything in the kitchen. I've got a telly, stereo, lots of books and magazines in the lounge."

Marcie was going to enjoy her stay in Judy's cozy little house. She almost cried when she entered her room and saw her belongings stacked in a corner, apparently undamaged.

"This is my son's room. He's visiting his grandparents for a fortnight."

"It's cute." She saw a child's drawing of a soccer ball pinned to a cork board. "Did he do this? It's very good. How old is he?"

"Seven. He loves sports, and he also likes to draw."

Below the drawing his name was spelled out in childish letters, which Marcie couldn't quite decipher. "What did you say his name is?"

"It's Dafydd. The Welsh version of David. Pronounced the same but with an *f* in stead of a *v*. His nickname is Dafe."

"Are you Welsh?" Marcie wasn't sure if she could tell a Scotts accent from a Welsh one.

"His father was Welsh."

Marcie caught the *was*. "I'm sorry."

"I lost my husband, Alistair, just over three years ago. We named Dafydd after Alistair's father. It means beloved." Judy moved to the bed and changed the subject. "I've put on fresh sheets. I hope you don't mind Star Wars. I've emptied two drawers and cleared half the closet."

"Thanks. You and Greg have been so generous. I don't know what I would have done without you or how I'll repay you."

"Just rest and get well. Do you need help unpacking?"

"No thanks. I can manage. I'm sure you need to get back to the office. Greg is probably lost without you."

"Yes, I think sometimes he is." Judy laughed.

They fell into easy conversation, like old friends, over tea and toast with butter and marmalade until Judy had to leave. "I'll be back about a quarter past six. Do as you wish. Make yourself at home. Do you like cats? I've a ginger cat about somewhere. Rumbles. He's good company, has a great purr, and loves a warm lap. Rest and I'll see you tonight."

Marcie didn't feel up to unpacking. She was tired and her arm ached. So she took off the sling and curled up on her bed with a book she found in the living room. *Himalayan Odyssey* was filled with stunning photographs.

***

Greg walked into Judy's office as soon as she returned from picking up Marcie. "Well?"

"She's a real sweetheart. We get on very well. She's like the sister I never had."

"You have a sister."

"Aye, but Marcie is like the one I never had: one I can get along with. I think she's a wee bit adrift."

"I think she's brave. We'd all be disoriented in the same situation." He leaned against the door jamb and slid his hands into his pants pockets, trying for a nonchalant attitude, when in fact he was worried and concerned and not sure what he should do about it. "You're back soon. Didn't you help her settle in?"

"Of course I offered. But she insisted I come back here. She thought you might be lost without me."

"I am. You know that." He should tell her more often.

"How long do you think she'll need to recover?" Judy sat before her computer and checked her e-mail.

"Do I hear regret?"

"No, no. I'm just wondering. If she's supposed to get well in a week or so but doesn't, then maybe something's wrong. Do I need to keep an eye out for symptoms? She had a pretty nasty bump to the head and I'm no doctor."

"Nor am I. They said she didn't have concussion so no problem there. I imagine she's supposed to go back for a follow-up. I guess we play it by ear."

***

After dinner, as Greg worked at his desk in his home study, he called Judy. "Marcie's settled in?"

"Why are you so concerned? I told you earlier she was."

"I just want to be sure you're okay having her stay with you. If it's too much trouble I can make other arrangements."

"Don't, she's fine here. When I got home and checked she was curled up on the bed sound asleep with the Himalaya book open beside her and Rumbles curled up next to her. Didn't take him long to warm up to her. I pulled the duvet over her and she's still asleep. Which is as it should be."

"Aye."

"Greg?"

"I'm still here."

"Why so much concern?"

He hesitated. But Judy knew him. And he knew Judy. She'd ask until she got an answer. And he wasn't so rude as to hang up on her, though he was tempted. "I'm responsible for her accident—"

"*Och* no, how can that be?"

"She was coming from a venue I suggested. If she'd stayed in Fort Augustus, as she'd planned, she wouldn't have been in the crash."

"That's ridiculous. You have to stop beating yourself up over Emma. It wasn't your fault."

"We're talking about Marcie," he said, his voice rougher than it should have been.

"Are we?"

Charming cottage home in Inverness, Scotland

CHAPTER FIVE

After a sound sleep uninterrupted by hospital routine, Marcie woke early feeling much more herself, and very hungry. She crossed the hall to the kitchen to make some tea and breakfast. The omelet, a bit tricky to make with one hand, looked more like scrambled eggs.

"That sure smells good." Judy stood in the doorway, wrapped in her robe and barely awake.

"I thought I'd make breakfast for you. Do you like omelets?"

"Luv 'em. I usually make do with tea and toast. This is a treat."

"I can make dinner, too. Just tell me what you would like and when you'll be home."

"Are you sure you're up to it?" Judy pulled plates from the cabinet and set the small bistro table in a corner of the kitchen. "I'm usually home about a quarter to six. I'd planned to use the

73

leftover chicken and rice in the fridge. It would just need reheating. I wouldn't want you to overdo it."

"Oh, I won't. I've got all day, haven't I? We could have dinner at 6:30. Or do you eat later? It's the least I can do to repay your kindness." She didn't want to be any trouble to Judy. She wanted to earn her own way, as she always had.

"Sevenish would be perfect. No need to do anything special. Don't tax yourself."

An hour later Judy left for work and Marcie was still cleaning up the breakfast dishes. The task took her twice as long as it should have because of her injury. But, as she reminded herself, she had all day.

She took a soothing soak in a hot bath and washed her hair, another challenge. Then set about straightening the rooms in the house. The house was clean and the furniture recently polished but newspapers, magazines and a sweater could be picked up so the house would look tidy when Judy came home.

As long as she didn't make any sudden moves her strains and bruises were tolerable.

After a long nap, with Rumbles purring beside her pillow, Marcie sat on a comfy sofa in Judy's living room with a few books. She picked guidebooks of the area she would travel in, when she could get back to it. The descriptions of forests, waterfalls, villages and castle ruins made her want to get out there and paint again. The first sprouts of frustration started to grow, and something worse, something dark and black she didn't want to face: the fear that it was over, that she would not be able to finish the job, that her dreams and plans would never be fulfilled.

She shelved the books and went to the kitchen where she started, slowly, to prepare the dinner. With her bandaged arm to hold things in place she used her left hand to chop and mix and spread. She added sliced carrots and peas to the chicken and rice, put it in a casserole dish with cream and cheese and spices, then covered it with a pastry crust. It wasn't as neat as she would have liked, but it would do. Once it went into the oven she started on a green salad. She was good at making a meal from whatever was at hand.

She set the table in the small dining room with a nice cloth from a cabinet in the corner. Crystal glasses from the same cabinet, and real silverware she found in the drawer, gave the table sparkle. Wildflowers from the garden, and her last freesia blossoms, added a welcome splash of color and fragrance. To play dress up, as it were, in a dining room with such beautiful things stirred longings in her for her own home and she imagined how she would decorate and furnish it. Whenever she let her imagination go in that direction, she imagined a loving husband and two or three children to fill the house. Always vague before, now the children had sandy hair and green eyes. What a hopeless dreamer she was.

In her room she looked through her clothes for something to wear. She hadn't brought much with her, but she had packed two dresses. The sundress she'd worn to the housewarming and a simple plum colored sheath in a fabric guaranteed not to wrinkle. When she put it on it didn't look as though it had been in her duffle for over a week. It fit her figure well. She brushed her hair until it hung in a shining curtain. It was difficult to pull the sides back and fasten them with barrettes and she got it crooked. Her bangs needed trimming but there was nothing she could do about that. Besides, they covered the bruise and stitches on her forehead. Makeup was tricky but it didn't really matter. Still, after looking at herself in the mirror, she had to at least try to do her eyes, to cover the black and blue, which was turning a yucky green and yellow. With a little makeup her eyes were actually pretty. And maybe… just maybe… Greg would come by.

Everything she'd done that day to pay her way, to show her gratitude to Judy—she had to admit to herself—wasn't totally done for that reason. A lot of it was for Greg, in hopes he would come by to see how she was feeling and be pleased to find her improving.

***

Marcie was ready and in the kitchen checking the casserole when she heard Judy's Fiat and another, deep-throated car come to a halt in the back. Then a man's voice. Marcie's heart raced. The door opened and Judy came in, followed by Greg.

"Hello, Marcie." Greg had to stoop to keep from hitting his head on the low cottage doorframe. "It's good to see you on your feet again." His tentative smile didn't quite reach his eyes as he looked at her and then took in the room. "Smells good."

He seemed upset. Her racing heart skipped with disappointment. She was a neat cook but in her present condition, she'd left a mess. Well, it couldn't be helped; she'd done her best.

Marcie caught Greg giving Judy a fleeting, irritated scowl. He was upset with Judy? Marcie wondered what was wrong between them. Maybe he hadn't wanted to come and Judy had forced him. *Forced him? I don't think so.* Then another thought chilled her like ice down her back, made her catch her breath: Maybe he and Judy were more then employer and employee. Maybe they were lovers. It was possible. Marcie turned away to check the casserole, then began to pull it from the oven. She could blame her flushed cheeks on the rising heat from the open oven door.

"Let me get that." Greg took the hot mitts and lifted the dish to the counter. "This looks delicious."

She breathed a sigh of relief at his smile. The tiff had passed, she guessed. She would watch them together, see if they were more than good friends. Better to know now and accept it than continue with foolish daydreams. "It needs to set for a few minutes. We can go to the living room. Would you like something to drink?" Marcie hoped Judy wouldn't think she was taking over her house. She just wanted show them both her gratitude.

"Yes, we'll have some cider and relax a bit first, scrumpy will be nice. I'll get it. Greg will help me." Judy reached into the fridge.

"Okay, I'll set another place at the table." Marcie went to the dining room, set the place, then headed for the living room. Greg was here for a dinner she'd cooked with him in mind. She shouldn't be so nervous. She was a good cook. She wanted to show him there was more to her than her art.

***

Greg was pleased to see Marcie but his gut tightened at the chaos in the kitchen. Not because he minded a mess, but because he minded Marcie doing all that work. He closed the kitchen door after she left for the dining room and turned to Judy. "What's—"

"I saw that look." Judy kept her voice low. "Don't dare think for one moment I put her up to this. She asked if she could make dinner. All I said was reheat the chicken and rice, not make a three-course meal."

"I'm sorry. I didn't really think you would take advantage. It's just she looks so tired." Pale and weary. So different from his rosy-cheeked, bright-eyed, eager-to-explore companion at Loch Leven. He could tell she'd tried to cover her bruises and pale cheeks with makeup. It touched him, made him want to take her in his arms and comfort her. He wanted to cosset her until she was well enough to paint again. But that was ridiculous. She was a grown woman able to take care of herself. If not, she wouldn't have been traveling halfway around the world on her own. If she felt well enough to cook supper, it was a good sign, wasn't it? It meant she was recovering and would soon be painting again.

They took the drinks to the lounge and Greg offered Marcie a glass, noticing a sparkle in her eyes. She *was* improved from when he'd visited her in the hospital. Soon she'd be well again.

"Thanks. Is this scrumpy?"

"Aye," Judy said. "Practically our national drink."

Marcie took a swallow then choked, spattering most of it onto her bandaged hand since her other hand still held the glass. She coughed and gasped.

"Careful, Marcie." Concerned, Greg sat next to her on the sofa and patted her back, then circled his hand over her shoulders. He liked the feel of her dress stretched over her firm, yet feminine curves. Her warmth soaked into his hand through the thin fabric. "You all right?"

She took a stuttering breath. "This is cider?"

"Aye. Apple cider, hard cider." Judy said taking the glass from Marcie and handing her some tissues.

Marcie mopped herself. "I'm so sorry, I've made a mess. Where I come from cider is apple juice. I wasn't expecting alcohol. Though it is kinda good, even if it did go up my nose."

She laughed and Greg was relieved. He admired her ability to laugh at herself. It hadn't occurred to him that Marcie wouldn't know what scrumpy was. He'd forgotten she'd been in Scotland only a fortnight or so, and it hadn't been served at Iona and Archie's housewarming. "Now that you know what it is, will you try it again?"

"No, thanks. I'm on meds. I don't think I'm supposed to mix them with alcohol."

"Very sensible," Greg said. "So, can we eat? I'm starved."

"Yes, of course. I've set the dining room. I found some nice things in the cabinet. I hope you don't mind, Judy."

"Not at all. It looks super. You'll spoil me." Judy said from the hall as she took their drinks to the dining room. Greg followed Marcie to the kitchen. She carried the salad and he followed with the casserole.

After serving everyone, Marcie sat. Greg noticed color had returned to her cheeks; she seemed happy. She always seemed happy, optimistic. He watched her dish up the casserole with her uninjured hand. "It's lucky you're left handed."

"But I'm not." Her smile faded.

For a moment Greg just looked at her. Then he realized what she meant. "*Ó, damnadh!* Don't tell me—" He remembered, when he'd found her on the Parade in Fort William, she had used both hands, her right to apply the watercolor with a brush, her left to dab it with toweling to get the effect she wanted. A cold knot formed in his gut and he swallowed some scrumpy to melt it. Otherwise he wouldn't be able to eat.

"Let's not talk about it." Marcie flashed her blue eyes at him.

"This is delicious," Judy said. "You made this from what I had in the kitchen?"

"It wasn't hard. I'm glad you like it." Her smile returned. Greg felt a desire to do whatever it took to keep her smiling, something he found so hard to do himself.

The savory scent of chicken and spices took his attention as he broke the flaky crust and loaded his fork. He was damn hungry and glad he had accepted Judy's invitation. The casserole was delicious. The crust was perfect, the filling creamy. It brought to mind potpies his mother had made when he was young. He wanted to ask Marcie how she managed with only one functioning hand, but she hadn't wanted to discuss her injury. And he didn't want that smile to disappear again, so he let it go.

Then another thought slammed in to him. How long before she could draw and paint again with an injury to her primary hand? Would she be able to continue? Was that why she didn't want to talk about it?

They had similar goals. Were both doomed?

***

The evening hadn't started out well, but as they talked and ate Marcie began to enjoy herself. Observing Greg and Judy, she came to the conclusion that the two were just good friends, and not lovers as she'd feared. That was enough of a relief for her to forget her troubles for an evening and enjoy Greg's company.

However, there was still one thing she needed and she screwed up the courage to ask. "Judy, do you have a computer I can use? I can't find my cell phone. I guess it was lost in the wreck. I don't seem to have very good luck with them. It's the second one I've lost since I got here. But I need to contact my father. And I want to email my friends."

"I don't have a computer. I'm on one all day at work and I don't want to do the same when I get home. I'll have to get one soon for Dafydd, but so far the school's computers satisfy him. I want to hold off getting him one as long as I can. Children grow up fast enough as it is."

"I understand. Is there an Internet café nearby?" She looked from Judy to Greg. She wanted to write to Wallie; she needed an outlet and Wallie was the safest.

"I have some redundant netbooks at the office," Greg said. "I'll bring one by tomorrow for your use."

"Thanks, Greg."

Relaxed now, Marcie enjoyed watching Greg eat the food she'd prepared. That she admitted to herself that she'd prepared in hopes he would come by to see her.

She felt bubbly in his company. Her heart danced when he was near. She was so captivated by him she had to remind herself not to stare. She wanted to memorize his face, his expressions, his nuances. Most of all she wanted him to notice *her*, to kiss her again.

***

Greg was well into sorting his day's workload the next morning when Judy arrived at the office. She brought him a cup of coffee and nothing else. She stood at his desk until he stopped what he was doing and looked up at her. She looked perturbed, or even worried.

"You want something?" he asked.

"What was all that at dinner last night?"

"I'm not sure I follow you."

"Marcie's hand. You said '*Ó, damnadh!*' like it had been cut off or something."

"Marcie is a incredibly talented illustrator. A right-handed illustrator."

"Right, you said she was what you were looking for for your new line of guides." Then she put a hand to her mouth. "*Och*, no. You mean she may never draw again? Do you know for sure?" Judy dropped into one of the chairs in front of Greg's desk.

"No, I don't know. But I saw it in her eyes, fear. She has expressive eyes, did you notice?"

"What are you going to do about it?"

"What do you mean, what am I going to do about it?"

"I just remembered. When I picked her up at the hospital I came into her room just as the doctor left. She was crying, quiet-like. Do you suppose he told her she would never draw again?"

"Don't be so dramatic! I don't know. I don't know a damn thing. Haven't you got something constructive to do? Are we all out of scones?"

"You're in a bad mood. You're usually so even tempered, it's almost as though you're worried about her. More so than a casual acquaintance would be, especially since Marcie has a contract with the competition."

"Sorry," was all he said even though he knew what was eating at him. It was discovering Marcie's art, finding her contracted to Caledon and Bishops, the hostile takeover, all in a few days.

***

After cleaning the breakfast dishes the next mooring, Marcie decided it was time to go for a walk and try to get over the lingering fatigue she'd felt since the accident. Greg had promised to bring her a computer. He'd probably stop by on his way home from work that evening. She didn't want to sit around all day waiting, anticipating his arrival, dreaming unlikely dreams. She needed to get out and move.

She shoved her wallet into a pocket and grabbed her camera. With the spare key Judy had given her, she made sure the door was locked, then turned toward the street. It was a nice, warm day. White, fluffy clouds ambled across a bright, blue sky. She took a deep breath of air scented with flowers and washed with a soft sea breeze.

Quaint houses and fascinating gardens slowed her progress as she strolled. She examined each garden: some gardens were wild like Judy's, others manicured and formal with little boxwood hedges.

Climbing roses covered stone walls, ivy rambled over brick. She looked at each one with her artist's eye. Windsor red and brown madder would be perfect for the aged bricks. Burnt umber and raw sienna to add texture and interest. French ultramarine for the shadows would make the colors pop. She envisioned watercolor paper filled with detailed snippets of bright flowers against mellowed brick and stone.

With her right hand cradled in her left, she tried to move her fingers as if holding a pencil or brush. Pain seared her arm and dread scorched her heart. She crossed the street and started back to Judy's, fighting the fear of her unknown future.

Her mind was busy with questions: How long could she take advantage of Judy's hospitality? When would she be able to draw and paint again? How would she be able to say good-bye? What would happen next?

She stopped at Judy's gate. Greg stood in the open doorway, dressed in another gorgeous business suit—the jacket was pushed back, his hands in his pockets—looking like her own *GQ* cover model.

"Did I forget to lock the door?" She was sure she had.

"I have a spare key."

"Oh. How long have you been waiting?"

"Not long. You're feeling better today."

"Yes. I thought a walk would help. I expected you to come after work. I'm sorry I wasn't here."

"Not a problem. I'm sure it must be claustrophobic spending the day in this little house."

"I love this house."

"I brought the computer for you. It's in the lounge. Let me show you." Greg made sure Marcie was familiar with the system, then handed her a cell phone. "Third time's a charm, don't you think?"

"Oh dear, do you trust me with it? Thanks, you're too generous."

He wished her a good day, then left. Too soon. Way too soon.

She stood in the doorway, as he had, and watched him drive away, then shut the door and returned to the computer to check her email.

> Marcie,
> That job is still open at the middle school, but I've heard there have been several applications. You know I'm happy to help finance your trip, as a graduation present, but I think your best bet is to apply for this job. I'll put in a good word for you.
> Dad

Marcie keyed in her reply, which was slow and frustrating and had to be in lowercase entirely since she could only use her left hand.

> hi dad.
> i'm on the fence about that job. give me another week to think about it, ok? i'll let you know.
> marcie

> wallie,
> hi. i need your medical advice. i was in a bit of an accident. no, i wasn't driving on the wrong side of the road. some other tourist was. i got a bit banged up. i'm worried about an injury to my right forearm. i know there's nothing you can do 7,000 miles away, i guess i just need to whine to someone. the doctor says i may not be able to draw again. but i'm not going to assume the worst. i'll be seeing a physical therapist soon. i don't mean to be a downer, it's just i need someone i can talk to.
> thanks for listening.
> bff, mw

        Marcie! I was just checking my email
before heading to bed. Just got off shift.
        Girl, what happened? Are you sure
you're ok? I wish I could examine your arm.
More details, please. If you're still online,
I'm here.
        Wallis

Marcie spent the next half hour online with Wallie, giving details, voicing concerns, until she took pity on her friend and let her get to bed. She felt much better having been able to talk through her fears with someone who would understand, but not try to make her change her plans. If her father knew of her injury, he'd try to persuade her to come home. Center City hadn't been her home since she'd gone off to college. She hadn't had a real home since her parents had divorced when she was twelve. They'd split their possessions and moved to new places and she'd never felt at home again as she'd been passed back and forth. She had always felt in the way. When she'd gone off to college, she'd vowed never to inconvenience her family again.

Because of that experience she knew she'd build a foundation of security for her children and they would always know they were loved, wanted and came first. That was why she wanted licensing. She'd be able to work from home and with a good contract she'd make a good living.

It made her sick to think of it, but she might have to apply for that job her father kept bringing up. If she could no longer paint, she could always teach. Just the thought was enough incentive to get well.

An email from Greg was at the bottom of her inbox. He'd sent it the morning of her accident. Her stomach fluttered with anticipation. She opened it.

        Hello Marcie,
        I got your text. I have a couple hours
free this morning. I'll find you and give you
more suggestions for places to paint. Maybe
we can fit in another walk.
        I look forward to seeing you again.
        Greg

> hi greg, i just found your email from last monday. i'd like to take you up on your invitation for another walk. maybe in a couple more days i'll be ready to go out somewhere.
>   i appreciate all you've done for me. this computer, judy's hospitality, have helped me cope with being so far from home.
>   most of all, thanks for being there when i wrecked the car. it really helped to have someone who cared by my side.
>   thanks. marcie

Saturday Marcie wrote out a menu for the week and she and Judy took her list of groceries to the local market. She enjoyed matching what she knew with what was available on the shelves. Some products were the same, some very different. They had fun, but the excursion tired Marcie and she spent the rest of the day curled up on the sofa reading Scottish magazines.

***

On Sunday Judy invited Marcie to go with her to St. Bridget's, the little stone church at the end of the street. It was a beautiful little church. It was also chilly inside; the thick stone walls kept out all of the summer sun's heat.

The fragrance of flowers, mixed with the musty scent of old wood, old fabrics, and the carbony smell of burning candles, brought to mind images of clans and chiefs, and kilted warriors with broad swords. She wanted to see Greg in a kilt again, just the thought warmed her.

As they walked home Marcie turned to Judy, hesitant to ask more favors but having no other options. "I have an appointment tomorrow with a therapist at two o'clock, and then I'm supposed to have a follow-up with the doctor. The therapist is located near the hospital. Could you tell me how to get there? Is there a bus?"

"I'll take you. I won't have you taking a bus or even a taxi."

"Will Greg mind if you take time off? I don't want to inconvenience you any more than I already have. You've been such a big help to me."

"He won't mind. He might even take you himself."

"On no, I couldn't let him do that," Marcie lied, though it was exactly what she'd like most.

"I'll take you to the office first and give you a tour. Would you like that?"

"Oh, yes! I'd love it. Especially the production of the books."

"Let's plan on it, then."

***

Greg was concentrating on a spreadsheet when Judy popped her head into his office on Monday morning with her usual greeting: "Good morning. Coffee?"

"Aye, thanks."

He looked up as the aroma of coffee and scones, warm and buttered the way he liked them, reached him. "Ah, you made scones." He knew she would. She always did.

"I didn't make them, Marcie did. You're allowed to say they're good, even as good as mine since I taught her how. But you're not allowed to say they're better." She put the tray on his desk.

"Then I'll just say thank you."

"Brilliant man."

He took a bite. They were perfect. "You want something?" He could tell she did by the way she lingered at his desk.

"Aye, I need to take a few hours off this afternoon."

"For what?"

"Marcie has an appointment with a therapist at a quarter past two. She seems a bit apprehensive about it so I thought I'd bring her here, give her a little tour. Then I'll take her to the therapist. It will help her relax before her appointment."

"A good idea. Yes, of course, you can take the afternoon off."

"Unless you need me for something *more* important, then you can take her."

What was she up to? She knew his schedule as well as he did. "I have a meeting with Mark at two to discuss his Alaska trip."

"Oh, I forgot to tell you. Celine is ill, Mark canceled."

"For goodness sake! Celine is a dog!" Greg picked up his coffee and sat back.

"And you wouldn't drop everything if Bobby was ill? Think about it. You have four hours to decide." Judy returned to her office.

Greg stared at the door. He didn't need to think about it. He would take Marcie to her appointment.

He opened his email and sent a message to Mark: *Sorry to hear Celine is ill. Let me know if I can do anyth*ing. *G.*

*Nessie, Loch Ness Monster sculpture at the Loch Ness Monster
Exhibition, Drumnadrochit*

CHAPTER SIX

Marcie was ready for Judy when she arrived soon after
lunch. Nervous, she hadn't been able to eat more than a few bites
of her salad. She checked herself in the mirror, smoothing the
sundress. She didn't cover the greenish splotch on her forehead
because the doctor would need to examine it. Instead, she combed
her bangs over it.

When they reached town, Judy pulled into a parking
garage below a modern building. They took an elevator up one
floor, but didn't go into the modern building; instead, they walked
along a corridor to the building next door. It was much older,
probably a couple of hundred years older. The lobby was paneled
in rich walnut wainscoting, the walls and ceiling above white
plaster. Large framed photographs of Inverness and Loch Ness
filled three walls. All were from different eras, some dating back to
early photography. Large gold letters above the reception desk
stated simply: McInnis House Press - 1887.

"This is really an impressive family business, isn't it?"
Marcie asked Judy.

"Passed from father to son for six generations. Greg's a direct descendant of the founder. Let's start on the top floor and work our way down. This way." Judy entered an elevator almost as old as the building.

"Wow, what a view!" Marcie said as she walked through a large comfortable break room to the windows. "You should have your office up here."

"It is nice, isn't it? I have a similar view from my office below."

Judy led the way to the next room. Marcie was impressed by the employee lounge, a full kitchen, and a gym with locker rooms and showers. Judy explained Greg had it built a couple of years before. What a great place to work and work out. They walked downstairs.

Marcie felt at home in the art department. She asked questions about the production of the books and examined the layout designs, dummies and storyboards pinned to the walls. The room was bright, open and airy with more large windows facing the river. There was a large, antique drawing table in one corner. But computer stations with large-screen monitors took up the rest of the space. She watched over one graphic artist's shoulder as she pulled in a photo, wrapped text around it, then added a drop cap.

Marcie could have spent all day in that room. She'd loved the graphic arts courses she'd taken in college. If she weren't so intent on being a licensed illustrator, she would love to work here. Perhaps, if she couldn't paint again… no, she wouldn't go there until she had to. But it was an option, which took some of the bleakness from her unknown future. More palatable than being an art teacher in a middle school in Center City, Nevada.

The art director, Anna McLoud, a small, plump woman in her fifties, welcomed Marcie with a warm smile and answered all her questions. They were instant friends.

Across the hall more graphic artists kept the company's web site up to date and fresh. She had to pull herself away, it was all so fascinating.

They walked through the editorial department, where she was introduced to several editors, assistants, secretaries and interns.

The more she saw, the more Marcie realized McInnis House Press was a thriving, prosperous business.

The hallways were decorated with framed covers from some of their publications and Marcie appreciated that Judy waited patiently while she examined each one.

When they entered Judy's office, Marcie went straight to the large photographs on the wall. "What spectacular photos! They're from the Himalaya book, aren't they?"

"Aye, our most extravagant publication to date. But tragic."

"How so?"

"After these pictures were taken the storm worsened. One member of the team died, the rest suffered varying degrees of frostbite."

"Oh, how awful." Marcie couldn't imagine such an ordeal. "Is that why Greg limps? Frostbite?"

"Aye. As leader of the expedition, Greg took it hard."

"I saw Greg's name on the book. I know he's a photographer but I didn't realize he was the leader, that he was one of the *professional* photographers. I thought he had something to do with planning and production."

Judy moved on to the next large photo. "This is one of his."

"Greg's? He took this? Wow, he really is good, isn't he?"

"Not quite as good as his father was but with time I think he'll exceed his father's reputation. Right now he's as good as Mark. Mark does the wildlife and Greg specializes in scenics."

"But he's in management, right? How will he have time to grow his skills if he has to spend all his time in the office?"

"I hadn't thought about that. We're still reeling from Greg's father's death. It was a hard blow to the company."

"I'm so sorry. Can you tell me about it?" Marcie wanted to know about Greg's family, she wanted to know the experiences that had formed him.

Judy sighed. "Three years ago, Greg's father, Gregor V, had this grand plan to photograph Everest and other mountains in the Himalaya from a level perspective. In other words, not looking up at them or down from them, but across to them. They had to climb to some fantastic heights to do that. Unfortunately, when they left the area, their plane went down killing all aboard and destroying all the images the team had taken."

Marcie put her hand to her throat. She couldn't imagine how anyone could survive such a loss, so many people must have been affected, family, friends, employees.

"You said someone died on Greg's expedition, too?"

"Emma, a gifted photographer. Greg's protégée. He feels responsible. It's been a difficult few years for him."

"Then I go and get in an accident and add to his troubles. I shouldn't bother him anymore with..."

An inner door opened and Greg stepped out, dressed in a beautiful gray suit with a light blue shirt and the gorgeous blue and green tartan tie she'd seen the day they'd met.

"What's wrong? Have I got my tie on wrong side out?" Greg looked down at his tie and tugged it in place.

"Oh no." Marcie felt hyperaware of him. The business man, a superb photographer, a man with many responsibilities. How had she ever entertained the idea that he could be interested in her for reasons other than her art? "I was just surprised you took these photos."

"Just a pastime. There's a change of plans. I need Judy to edit some urgent reports and my meeting has been canceled. So I'll take you to your appointment."

"Okay." Marcie tried to act casual about it when inside she trembled with excitement and uncertainty, which obliterated the apprehension she'd felt about her appointment.

"You've had your tour?"

"Yes. I'm impressed. You have a lot of talented people working here."

"Aye, we do." Greg held the door open. They walked down to the underground garage and Greg stopped beside a classic-era, royal blue Rolls Royce and opened the passenger door.

Marcie stared. "This is a Rolls Royce. You have a Land Rover."

"I do have a Land Rover. This was my father's car. It's more appropriate for business. Get in. It won't bite."

Marcie slid in over the leather seat and ran her fingers over the polished wood dash. She watched Greg as he rounded the car and got in beside her. All confident and business-like. Where was the wind-blown, mischievous, bad boy, who had shared his fish and chips in the park, and taken her to Grey Mare Falls? Suddenly he was head of a very successful family business, who drove expensive cars and wore expensive suits.

"Fasten your seat belt." He started the engine.

"I can't reach it with my left hand." She probably could if she wanted to, but she didn't want to.

Greg reached over her and pulled the belt to the latch. The clean fragrance of his hair and woodsy aftershave was almost too much. She had to get a grip, or she wouldn't be coherent at her appointment. The thought of that ordeal sobered her enough to forget fantasies about the man seated next to her. In a Rolls Royce!

***

Marcie waited as Greg unlatched her seat belt when they arrived at the medical building, then came around the car to open her door. He was such a gentleman.

"I'll go in with you, if you like," Greg said when they reached the therapist's office.

"I can use the moral support." It was exactly what she wanted. If it was bad news, she'd need Greg there so she wouldn't lose it. Because she could never do that in front of him.

As they waited, Greg talked about photographic trips he'd taken, keeping her entertained and distracted. He was a good storyteller, making her laugh at some of his youthful antics. He didn't mention the Himalaya trip, and she didn't ask.

When it was her turn, they were led into a small exam room. The therapist introduced himself and agreed Greg was welcome to sit and observe.

"First, let's take off the elastic wrap," the therapist said. He took her arm gently in his hands and began to unwrap the bandage. Even though he was careful the shock of his touch was painful and made her pull in a breath. She'd changed the bandage herself each day but somehow, having someone else do it was excruciating.

"You've an appointment to see the doctor soon?" he asked.

"Yes. After this. A follow-up to check the wound and stitches."

"Stitches? Lord, Marcie!" Greg said as the reddened, ragged gash on her arm was revealed. "They said a laceration. I had no idea it was so serious."

"Oh, I thought you knew." Marcie looked at Greg, then back at her arm. The therapist continued his examination. Her heart pounded. Greg's genuine concern indicated he thought the wound shocking. Maybe the injury was worse than she'd thought.

"We'll discard the elastic wrap and splint and I'll give you a brace you're to wear until further notice," the therapist continued. "Dr. MacFarren has sent your records and X-rays. The injury is mainly to the extensor digitorum and the two lesser muscles on either side. In other words, the muscles that run from your elbow to your hand and control your fingers. You're lucky they were not severed. However, it will take time and patience to regain control. I understand you're an artist? You should be able to draw and paint again within a few months. Less if you follow instructions and do your exercises."

"I will! I will! You really think I'll paint again?" Marcie shot Greg a big grin then turned back to the therapist. Her heart hammered in her chest.

"I see no reason why not. Just be careful at first. Until the muscles have healed, they're susceptible to tearing if you try to go at it too quickly."

Marcie felt an immense relief from a fear she hadn't wanted to acknowledge but knew had been a possibility. She *would* paint again.

The therapist tested Marcie's flexibility and control and she was shocked that she had little of either. Her hopes plummeted again. He didn't seem concerned as he showed her how to do some simple exercises, how to place the brace. He gave her padding to protect the wound.

While Marcie was taken to the reception desk to finish her paperwork and to pick up a printout of instructions for her exercises, Greg stayed behind and talked to the therapist. Was he asking about her future as a commercial artist? Marcie wondered. Because if the therapist told Greg she'd not be as good as before the accident, Greg might just lose interest in her.

And that would break her heart.

***

Greg helped Marcie into the Rolls. Her reaction to it had been just as he'd thought it might be. She appreciated the luxury, but preferred the Land Rover. He preferred it, too.

He drove a short distance to the hospital outpatient wing. "Are you nervous about this appointment?"

"I was more nervous with the therapist. I think he might be a better judge of how much control I'll be able to recover. I hope the doctor will take the stitches out because they're starting to itch."

It had almost made him sick when he'd seen Marcie's injury exposed. And he had a strong stomach. It wasn't so much the injury itself as the realization how close she'd come to losing the use of her hand completely, never able to draw again.

She seemed upset now even though the news had been good. "Something's bothering you."

"Maybe it's time I go home."

He felt her frustration, her doubt. "Why don't you stay for a while and see what happens? Wait to see what Mr. Fairmont has to say." He didn't want her to bolt. He wanted her to stay until the Caledon and Bishops acquisition process was settled, if it could be done before his deadline. By then he was sure he could win over his grandfather and his uncle, and offer Marcie a contract, either for the original project or something new, something exciting that would showcase her talent. He wanted to believe her talent would survive.

"I shouldn't spend any more money without knowing if I'll earn it back. I can't stay with Judy much longer. Her son will be home soon and he'll want his room back."

"We'll work something out if it comes to that. We want to see you successful. I think your art is perfect for licensing."

"Licensing?"

When she turned her bright eyes to him, something caught in his throat. His heart?

"That's my goal, to license my illustrations."

"Have you had any success?" Did she already have a contract for licensing as well?

"My contract with Caledon and Bishops includes limited licensing after publication." She turned back in her seat, worry creasing her brow again. "I still haven't heard from Mr. Fairmont.

christy olesen

I was supposed to meet him in Glasgow in a couple days for a
progress report. I guess I could still do that, though I dread telling
him I've had a set back."

"Here we are." He pulled up near the hospital entrance, got
out and opened her door. He sensed her tense as he leaned in to
unlatch her seat belt and thought perhaps she didn't like needing
help from others. The surprising thing was, he liked helping her.
"Wait for me inside while I park the car."

As he looked for a spot, found it and walked back to the
hospital, he tried to come up with some logical reason why Marcie
shouldn't go to Glasgow where she would be sure to find out her
contract was now in limbo.

He joined her in the lobby with no answer to his problem
and they walked to the outpatients' waiting room.

Now he couldn't wait until McInnis House Press took over
Caledon and Bishops. Sacking Farimont was the first thing he
would do. Why couldn't the man return Marcie's calls and emails?
Tell her what was happening?

"I've decided," she said, surprising him with her vim. "I'll
stay and do my best to finish what I've started."

"I'm glad to hear it. A week ago your world was turned
upside down. It will take some time and patience to turn it right
side up again, but you're clever, I'm sure you'll do it."

"They're calling my name. Please, come with me."

The appointment took no time at all. The stitches on her
forehead were removed and the wound examined. The swelling
and bruising were gone. The stitches in her arm would have to stay
another week.

The doctor asked a few questions and was satisfied with
Marcie's answers. "I see no reason why you shouldn't travel home
when you originally planned. Continue with the exercises and ask
your doctor at home to recommend a therapist who can take over
your treatment. Travel as light as you can. Ship home what you
don't need to carry. Continue to use the sling for another week or
so."

"You've had good news from both the therapist and the
doctor," Greg said as they walked to the Rolls. "We'll go
somewhere to celebrate."

"I'd like that."

"I'd like to take you to an old fashioned tea. I know just the place." He was rewarded with her bright smile. For that he'd suffer the teashop's frilly, fussy atmosphere.

"Thanks for doing this for me. I mean, bringing me, and sitting with me. You've made it more, I don't know, comfortable, I guess."

Her sincere gratitude warmed him. It also made him feel duplicitous. Was he helping her because she needed it? Or because he wanted to keep an eye on her, so he could grab her—and her artwork—when Celedon and Bishops cut her loose? Or was he helping her because he was growing to care for her?

But what did he have to offer her? He still hadn't convinced his grandfather and Rowan that using watercolor illustrations would be a smart addition to the business. Without their backing he had nothing to offer Marcie.

***

Marcie watched Inverness recede in the side mirror as Greg drove through the city and into the country. The road hugged the Loch Ness shoreline. She'd missed this area because the accident had happened before she'd gotten this far along her route. The black cloud that had hung over her since the day in the hospital when the doctor had said she might never draw again had lifted. She felt almost light-headed with relief.

Loch Ness was long and narrow. The water was dark like all the other lochs she'd seen in the Great Glen. The cerulean sky was banded with the fast moving clouds she'd come to expect. The mountains were lower here than in the West but just as green and just as old.

Would she be able to finish the project? Her emotions had spiked up and down so much in the last few hours she was worn out, didn't know what to think.

"Marcie? What's wrong?" Greg slowed the car.

She'd been looking out the passenger window, so caught up with her troubles she hadn't heard him speak. He put a hand on her shoulder, his tenderness gaining her attention. She wanted his arms around her, wanted to be blanked in his warmth, comforted when her dreams were evaporating. She wanted him to make all the pain go away. Which was ridiculous. It was her life, her job, her problem.

"Nothing." She took a deep breath, then turned and saw how worried he looked. He deserved an explanation. "I was just thinking, even if I stay until my original departure date, there's no way I'll be able to finish the job this year. I'll have to come back next summer... Pull over, please. I need to get out."

The road was narrow, following close to the loch. "There's a lay-by further on. Will that do?"

"Yes." The Rolls was big but she felt trapped, suffocated. She needed to get out, get away, as panic gripped her. It was all clear now. Even if she might draw and paint again, there wasn't enough time to do this job, which was her dream job, the ticket to her dream career, the step she needed to get the attention of Amanda Roth. She'd been lucky to get the chance once; a second chance might never come.

Greg's brows gathered with worry and concern and she felt bad for casting a shadow on his day, after he'd been so kind to take her to her appointments and now to tea.

He pulled off the road and she tried to unlatch her belt. He turned in his seat and reached for the latch. He was so close he could probably hear her heart pounding. With fingers on the latch he just looked at her, causing her breath to stall in her throat. She could feel that connection again. She could see the gold flecks in his green eyes and when they dropped to her mouth she involuntarily moistened her lips, tasting salty tears.

But he didn't kiss her. *He didn't kiss me.*

"How old are you, Marcie?" He pulled a handkerchief from his breast pocket and reached to wipe her tears. She took it from him and dabbed her own eyes and cheeks, shamed by her weakness.

"I'm twenty-six. Why?"

"Nothing, it's just that sometimes you look about eighteen."

Is that why he hadn't kissed her? He thought she was too young for him? Too immature? He hadn't thought that at Loch Leven. "How old are you?"

"Thirty-three."

"That old, huh? Let me call the rest home." Joel was twenty years older than she and that had never stopped him. Remembering Joel ratcheted her cranky mood up another few notches. "I need to get out. Now. Please." She shoved the handkerchief back in his pocket.

He unlatched her seat belt, and she pushed the door open, then marched to a retaining wall that overlooked the loch and lifted her face to the breeze. It was soft on her heated cheeks. Soft and fragrant, carrying the scent of damp earth and the plants that grew in it, the scent of water, fresh and clean. In the distance gulls scratched the sky with their black-tipped wings. A motorboat cruised past, and geese bobbed on its wake.

Why hadn't he kissed her? More to the point, why hadn't she kissed him? He'd been so close, she could have reached up and... But, if he hadn't kissed her back... The rejection would be too humiliating to bear. At least this way she could still dream of possibilities, remember the kiss they had shared at the falls.

Her arm ached from the exams. She slipped it from the sling, raised both arms high above her head—stretching her left arm fully and her right arm gingerly—arched her spine and let her head fall back. Eyes closed, she tried to relieve the tension coiled tightly in her body.

"Are you reaching for the stars?"

Marcie jumped at Greg's voice so close. Dropping her arms, she turned and bumped right into his solid chest. His arms wrapped around her, pulling her close. His eyes searched hers, as if he sensed the same connection she'd felt since they first met. Then his eyes dropped to her mouth.

She had a second chance.

She could barely breathe. Her heart danced to a new rhythm. She wrapped her hand around his tartan tie and tugged until he lowered his head. Then she pushed up on her toes and kissed him. This time it wasn't a tentative first kiss between near strangers, but one between friends exploring the promise of becoming lovers. He surrounded her. Her skin tingled where his hands caressed her back. One large hand dropped to brand her bottom, pulling her softness against his solidity. As the kiss moved quickly from query to enthusiasm, his other hand threaded through her hair to cup the back of her head. She felt encased in his warmth. The tension of a moment ago melted into a pool of exquisite heat. Everything that wasn't Greg's lips or hands or solid chest, fell away. There were no problems, no accident, and no possible end to her career before it had begun. Just Greg's strong arms wrapping her in his welcoming embrace. Just Greg's lips caressing and searching hers. Just the connection she'd felt all along, finally fulfilled.

She moaned with pleasure…

He broke the kiss and held her at arm's length.

Stunned, Marcie blinked against the light.

"Did I hurt you?"

Not hardly! Then Marcie realized Greg was talking about her injured arm, which had been pressed between then. She'd forgotten it. It ached from his embrace, now that she thought about it, but she'd squish it between them again if it meant Greg would put his arms around her and touch her as he just had. "I'm fine." *More than fine.*

"I promised you tea." His words were spoken as if they hadn't just shared an epiphany of a kiss. But his expression was adorably confused.

Greg opened the car door, waited until she was settled, then leaned in to fasten her belt, doing untold damage to her already shredded composure.

***

Greg was a first-rate multi tasker. Right now, as he walked down the hall to his office—excruciatingly aware of Marcie by his side—part of his brain… er, body… still buzzed from that *kiss*. Had he kissed her or had she kissed him? Once she'd turned into his arms he'd been lost to the feelings, her lushness, her softness.

He should have had more control, but she'd looked so vulnerable with her arm in the brace, so sexy reaching her hands to the heavens, her dress stretching against her curves. He'd wanted those curves pressed against him. She'd seemed so alone; he'd wanted to reassure her. But he'd allowed his sensibility to lapse and his senses to take over and he'd pulled her close. Too close.

He wouldn't let it happen again. Couldn't. It wouldn't be fair to her. He couldn't give her what she deserved emotionally. But hopefully he could give her what she needed to start her career.

Another part of his brain tried to sort out her mood as it swung from doubt to hope to defeat. How could he help her?

Before they reached his office, he had a solution to the problem of how to keep her from going to Glasgow where she was sure to find chaos at the offices of Caledon and Bishops. He'd clear his schedule and go himself.

"I'm going to Glasgow on business for a couple of days. I can look up Mr. Fairmont and find out why he hasn't returned your calls."

She stopped and turned to him. "I wouldn't want to inconvenience you."

"It's no problem, Marcie. I'm happy to do it. I have to go anyway." Another lie.

"Then I'd appreciate it if you could see him. Tell him I still want to do the project if he can wait until I'm able. And ask him to please call me."

"I promised to bring Bobby over one day. Can you take care of him while I'm gone? He's better company than Rumbles. You can take him for walks."

"I'd love to have him. Judy won't mind? It won't upset Rumbles?"

"Judy often takes Bobby when I go out of town." Pleased that was settled, Greg urged Marcie on to his office and excused himself to speak to one of the editors hovering in his doorway.

***

A few minutes later Greg walked into Judy's office and was taken aback by how the cozy the two women were. Marcie had been living with Judy for less than a week, yet they appeared to be long-time friends. It pleased him to see two women he cared for becoming close. Marcie was telling Judy about her appointments. Greg stopped inside the door, not wanting to interrupt, wanting to observe, to see if Marcie would be more open with her concerns to Judy.

"The therapist says with time and some exercises I will recover," she said. "But I don't think that will happen in the next four weeks. And if it did, I wouldn't have enough time to complete all the contracted paintings before I have to return home."

"Can't you stay longer? Through July, even into August?"

"I'm afraid my money would run out before then. I've saved a lot staying with you. But since you won't take the room and board I offered I don't feel right staying any longer, especially with your son coming home soon. And my tickets home are non-refundable, I can't afford new tickets and…"

Greg could feel Marcie struggle with her dilemma and wanted to step in and take care of everything for her, but he had to stand back and let her make her own choices.

"Do you need to make a decision now?" Judy said. "Why not think about it for another week. When Dafydd comes home, we'll figure out something for you." Judy noticed Greg then and gave him a pointed look.

"Okay, I'll give it another week. I had been afraid I was done for good, but now I'm excited about the therapist's prognosis. He believes I'll be able to paint again."

"That's great news. We should celebrate," Judy said.

"Greg treated me a wonderful tea in Drumna…Drumna…"

"Drumnadrochit. I know the place, all lace and china and delicious cream cakes." Judy gave Greg another pointed look.

He'd taken Judy to the same teashop once for her birthday. He'd hated the place. They had joked about it later and he'd said he would never go there again. Yet he'd taken Marcie there today. Because he thought she'd enjoy it. It hadn't been so awful.

Marcie turned and smiled at Greg and he felt it go straight to his heart.

"Mark wants you to come over tonight," Judy said. "Something about brilliant photos from his Alaska trip."

"You and Marcie, too, of course," Greg said.

"Not me, but Marcie should go." Judy turned to Marcie. "Would you like to see Mark's Alaska photos?"

"Yes, I'd love to."

"Good," Greg said. "I'll pick you up around half past six." Greg turned to Judy. He could read the warning in her eyes but didn't heed it. "I'm sure you'd enjoy the photos, too, Judy. Please, join us."

"You have a meeting in five minutes with Mr. Murphy. He's probably on his way up as we speak. I'll take Marcie home."

Marcie and Judy turned to go but Greg held Judy back with a hand on her arm. "Give me one reason why you won't go with us to Mark's."

"He's not my type."

"You—"

"Before you give me a lecture, it's not a racial thing."

"I wasn't thinking that. I know you don't have prejudices. I just don't understand why you won't go to his home to see his photos. You don't have to like the lad to appreciate his work."

"I do appreciate his work. He's good. He's also conceited and flirtatious. I'll see the shots when they go into production."

"Then you'll miss the raw, unedited images. I want your input on what to include in the book." Greg dropped his hand and Judy followed after Marcie. "If you gave him a chance, you'd like him." He wouldn't play matchmaker, but he still thought Judy and Mark would be good together. It was time Judy stepped out of her grief-created shell. He knew how painful it was to lose someone close, but it shouldn't cloud the rest of her life.

God, who was he to give advice?

Yet he couldn't help thinking it would help his social life if his friends liked each other. Did he have a social life? At that moment Mr. Murphy stepped through the door and Greg gave him his undivided attention.

***

That evening, Marcie stood in the doorway to Judy's living room. "Sure you won't go with us? It would make a nice foursome."

"Positive. I've got stuff to catch up on." Judy looked at her watch. "I'll be calling Dafydd in an hour or so. I try to call him each night at bedtime." She was curled up on her sofa with a novel. "Have a good time. You've got your key?"

"Yes. Thanks." Marcie opened the door just as Greg reached it. He'd changed into jeans and windbreaker. *Her* Greg again.

"You're in for a treat tonight, Marcie. Mark is an exceptional photographer. Have you been to Alaska?" He held the car door open for her and reached in to buckle her belt.

She closed her eyes and leaned her head back. This was too close for comfort. What had he just said? Oh, yeah. "No, I've never been. I've wanted to. Maybe Mark will have some pointers on the best places to visit." She relaxed as Greg stepped in his own side and pulled away from the curb.

"I'm sure he will. There's something… I mean, I think I should warn you…" He was quiet while he negotiated traffic, though Marcie was sure he knew the city well enough to drive through it and hold a conversation at the same time. "On the Himalaya trip Mark suffered from frostbite. He lost some fingers and toes. But he's adapted, learned to work with what he has. He hasn't lost his sense of humor or his drive to be 'the best wildlife photographer in the world'. His words."

"I look forward to meeting him. I can't imagine going through something like that. I'd like to know how he coped. Injuries like that might have ended his career, his art. Do you think he'd mind me asking?"

"Mark is not shy."

They parked on the street and walked to a row house converted to apartments. Mark's was on the third floor. Marcie noticed that although Greg had no trouble climbing the stairs, his limp was more pronounced. She wondered how his injuries had affected him. She suspected it wasn't the physical injuries that had hurt the most, but the danger his team had been in. The loss of a team member must have been unbearable.

Mark opened the door before Greg had a chance to knock. "Greg, glad to see you, mate," Mark said with a strong Jamaican accent. He turned sparkling, coal black eyes to Marcie.

"This is Marcie Winters, from the States," Greg said. "She's a brilliant artist."

"Glad to meet you, Marcie. Come in." Mark welcomed Marcie like one in a group of old friends with an enthusiastic hug. She liked him at once.

Not as big as Greg, Mark was still tall and athletic. His olive skin was smooth; he had a short beard, which he said he'd grown while in Alaska. His hair was black, curly, and worn a little long. His nose was broad above a wide mouth. He smiled often, revealing straight white teeth and a dimple in his cheek. Even his eyes smiled.

His smile dimmed when he looked past them. "Judy didn't come?"

"She had to call her son," Marcie said, forgetting for a moment that Judy was Greg's assistant and friend and he should probably be making her excuses for her.

"Well, her loss." Mark's smile came back full force, but Marcie could see disappointment in his eyes. And she noticed his accent was now more American. She had an idea that Mark could be whoever he wanted to be at any given moment.

Marcie noticed Mark's injuries. He was missing the ends of two fingers on his right hand and his pinky on his left. He limped, too, more so than Greg. Yet he didn't seem self-conscious about it.

Dinner was fresh Pacific salmon, which Mark had caught the day he'd left Anchorage.

The building was on a bluff and the dining room window overlooked the city. Marcie had a hard time dividing her attention between two handsome men, a fantastic view and a delicious dinner.

After dinner Mark connected his digital camera to a large screen TV. "This is going to be rough. I took over 2200 photos in two weeks! The weather was perfect. Hang on and have patience while I pick out the best."

Magnificent shots of caribou, Dall sheep, moose, and delicate miniature alpine wildflowers were interspersed with breathtaking shots of majestic mountains, their tops shrouded in mist and cloud, all on a much larger scale than the Highlands, or even the Sierra Nevada Marcie knew so well. All the while Mark entertained them with his narrative.

Marcie sat on the small sofa close to Greg. Really close. In fact, so close he soon put his arm over the sofa's back and rested his hand on her shoulder. His thumb made slow circles against her neck, under her hair. The tender, intimate touch just about distracted her from the images on the TV monitor. One or two of her sighs weren't responses to the photos.

Mark sat on her other side, controlling the images on the screen, and she felt as if he was giving her a personal tour of the Alaskan wilderness.

"Of course," Mark said, "two weeks isn't near long enough. I met a couple, both photographers. They've lived there for 20 years and are still excited to photograph the region. Greg, you've got to go to Denali Park and shoot Mt. McKinley. You've never seen anything like it. So different from Everest."

"It will have to wait. There's too much going on now."

"Oh, right," Mark said. "The hostile takeover. How's that "

"Let's not talk shop," Greg said with a rough and commanding tone as he leaned over Marcie and gave Mark a warning look. Marcie wondered what that was about. "You free for a few weeks?" Greg continued.

"I haven't booked anything. You want me to start the edit on the Alaska photos, right?"

Greg handed Mark a photo card. "Aye, and I need you to edit these I took for the Cairngorm book we talked about. Edit the Alaska photos with a calendar and such in mind, too."

"You do licensing?" Marcie asked Mark. "That's my goal, a good licensing contract." The evening was getting better.

"You don't have that with Caledon?" Greg asked.

"Yes, but it's limited to paper goods: calendars, note cards. No textiles, ceramics or plastics. It's a good start though." She turned back to Mark. "Do you do much licensing?"

"God, yes. It's about half my income right now, and climbing."

Marcie picked up the mug she'd been served coffee in. "This is yours, isn't it?" She turned it around to look at the photo of wildflowers.

"Yeah, I wouldn't own coffee mugs with flowers on them unless I took the shots." He turned when a high-pitched whine sounded from behind them. "Mind if I let my dog in? I had to shut her in the bedroom when I was cooking the salmon. She was drivin' I nuts." Mark said the last with a heavy Jamaican accent.

"Please do. I love dogs," Marcie said.

With a wink and a smile Mark left the room and came back with a large black Labrador at his heels. Mark sat and the dog greeted them with a wagging tail and cold wet nose before she plopped down at his feet.

"How is Celine?" Greg asked.

"She's fine."

"Judy said she was ill, that's why you canceled our meeting today."

"Oh. Right. She called. I mean, I called her. It was just a fur ball or something."

Marcie got it, if Greg didn't. Judy must have called Mark to ask him to cancel their meeting so Greg would be free to take her to her appointments. A mischievous twinkle in Mark's dark eyes led Marcie to believe she'd guessed right.

"I never heard of a dog having fur balls." Greg looked at Marcie.

"Don't look at me. I've never owned any dogs." The look on Greg's face made her giggle. He looked puzzled, as though he'd been left out of a private joke. When Mark laughed with her, they both were wiping tears from their eyes before they could stop.

They sat on the sofa until late, just talking. Mark popped a DVD into the player under the TV monitor and opened it to more photos he'd taken. Marcie could sit there all night looking at Mark's work. With Greg, his arm now relaxed, heavy and warm on her shoulder, holding her close to his side, it was a perfect evening.

Mark showed images he'd taken when he'd visited his grandmother in Jamaica. The lush tropics and turquoise sea were a stark contrast to the Alaska photos. He switched to photos taken in the Himalaya, shots not included in the book. She learned more about their trip. From Mark, not Greg. Mark seemed to need to talk about it, while Greg tensed, pulled his arm away and looked at his watch.

"I can't imagine how you survived the storm," Marcie said. The first photos, when the weather had been ideal, were gorgeous. The last photos they had taken before they had to pack away their camera gear, to keep it safe while they tried to survive, were awe inspiring in showing the storm's sheer power.

"We didn't. Not all of us," Mark said, serious for the first time since she'd met him. "It changed us."

Greg stood. He looked at her and she could tell the memory was painful. "Time to go, Marcie. It's almost two."

"Two! No way." She turned to Mark. "This has been so much fun, thanks for showing me your photographs. You're an excellent photographer, probably the world's best."

"That's what I keep telling everyone. I want to see your watercolors. You should have brought them with you tonight."

"I'm sorry, I didn't even think of it. Can I ask you, how did you adjust to your injuries?"

"It was difficult at first, I won't deny it. There were dark days when I thought I would have to go on the dole. Greg told me about your accident. I want you to know you *will* come back. It's frustrating, learning something over that once was second nature to you, but it can be done."

"That's just what I needed to hear. Coming from you it means so much." She reached up and kissed his cheek. He gave her a hug, walked them to the door and wished them good night.

***

At Judy's front door Marcie turned to Greg. "Thanks for this evening. I loved Mark's photos. And I enjoyed meeting him. He's funny, a real character."

"He's a good mate."

She pulled her key from her pocket and fiddled with it. When he didn't say more or move closer, she claimed newfound courage, reached up, and with one hand on his cheek, kissed him— a chaste, goodnight kiss. Her fingers tingled as they rasped against his two a.m. whiskers. But if the kiss was to be more, he'd need to make the next move. She could put herself out there only so far. When he didn't, she stifled her disappointment. "I'd like to see more of your photos sometime." She took a chance, inviting herself into his life. She wanted to know more about him, she wanted to be closer, but her courage wouldn't quite stretch that far. He'd have to meet her halfway.

"Just look on Judy's bookshelves. You'll see all the photos I've taken worth viewing. Now go on in, get some rest. It's late."

It wasn't until she was inside and had bolted the door that she heard his footsteps on the pavement and his car start up and move off.

Urquhart Castle ruins on a misty day at Loch Ness

CHAPTER SEVEN

The next morning Greg started the coffee while he waited for Judy. When she arrived he met her at the door. "I didn't have a chance to talk to you alone yesterday before you took Marcie home. Have you seen her injury?"

"Good morning to you, too. No, she always has it covered. What's wrong?" She put her things away and walked to the coffee maker.

"I thought she had a bad sprain. They said laceration. But what's a laceration? A cut, a scratch? She has a nasty, jagged rip across her arm that almost severed the muscles that control her fingers. I didn't notice it when I pulled her from the car. I thought the blood was from her head wound."

"Oh dear. And I let her do all that cooking."

"She told me she'd been frightened she wouldn't be able to paint at all. I'm afraid she never will."

"She said the therapist said she would." Judy leaned back against the counter to wait for the coffee to finish brewing.

"You should have seen how little control she has. I'm sure she has no other training. How will she support herself?" Agitated, he paced the office. "It's hard enough to make a living as an artist, and she had the potential to make a good living with the right marketing."

"If the therapist said she'll draw again, he would know, wouldn't he? She told me this morning Mark gave her an encouraging talk last night. It lifted her spirits."

"Aye, he was in good form." Last night, for the first time, Greg had lost patience with Mark's flirtatious nature. He'd almost pulled Mark aside to tell him to take it down a notch. But what right had he to do that? He had no claim on Marcie.

"Mark's a flirt." Judy poured mugs and handed one to Greg, then pointed to the sack she'd brought in.

"He likes people." Greg didn't want another Mark argument. He wasn't even sure whose side he was on now.

He went into his office and stared out the window, thinking about Marcie, examining his feelings for her. He wanted to see her become a successful artist. He wanted to help her with her career.

What *was* Marcie to him?

Was she his protégée? Could he handle having another protégée after failing Emma so spectacularly?

***

"Boss?" Judy said the next morning when she brought in his mail.

"Boss? You want something." He wasn't sure he wanted to hear what she had to say. She had that determined, you-know-what-you-should-do look.

"Have you told Marcie about McInnis' plan to buy out Caledon and Bishops?"

"No. Have you?"

"No, of course not. I know the policy. So, she has no idea her contract with them could be canceled?"

"She's not the only one." He held up a handful of papers that had nothing to do with Caledon but would help him make his point. "Here's a list. Want me to call them all?"

"Of course not," Judy said.

"I have to wait until the deal's done, until she's better. Recovered."

"She deserves to know. She has that right."

"She pretty much thinks it will be canceled because of her injury. She doesn't need to worry that it will be a casualty of the hostile takeover."

"There must be something we can do? What about your presentation?"

"I can't offer her anything until I clear it with Granddad. Every idea I have, I now have to clear with him. After the Himalaya expedition he doesn't trust me not to screw up."

"I'm sorry. If it helps, I believe in you and your idea. I think it's brilliant."

"Thanks. I'm glad to have you on my side." He picked up his briefcase and headed for the door. "I'm on my way to Glasgow, a last minute meeting. I've cleared my calendar. I'll be back Thursday morning."

"You're going to Caledon and Bishops? What for? I didn't hear about any meetings?"

Greg walked past Judy to the outer door. He hated how the lies were stacking up, but he couldn't seem to stop them. Each one should be temporary and explainable at a later date, but he wasn't secure in that assumption anymore. He trusted Judy, so he wasn't sure why he didn't want to tell her his real reason for going to Glasgow. She would read too much into it, that's why. "See you day after tomorrow." He stepped through the door, stopped and turned back. "I'm taking Bobby to Marcie. She'll watch him while I'm gone." To evade more questions, he hurried down the hall as though he were late for those fictitious meetings.

***

After the late night out, Marcie barely woke in time to fix breakfast for Judy. After Judy left, she fed Rumbles, then went back to bed. When she woke again the whole day stretched before her. Empty. With her appointments over, and the doctor's approval that she could travel, she had a big decision to make.

She would curl up on the sofa with some tea and think through all her options. Since her robe was short and lightweight— more a beach wrap than a robe, easy to pack—she grabbed a throw from Judy's linen closet to take with her to the living room. A scone with her tea would be a comfort, too.

Marcie jumped and let out a shriek when she entered the kitchen and found Greg just inside the back door. Her heart raced, more from the sight of him than the scare he'd given her. Raindrops sparkled in his hair and beaded on his waterproof jacket. He seemed so tall, his head nearly touching the low ceiling. A bundle of toweling—Judy's kitchen towel she noticed—wiggled in his arms.

"Sorry, didn't mean to startle you." He bent and Bobby hopped out of the towel and headed straight for Rumbles, who tensed, then ignored him with that royal attitude cats do so well.

She dropped the throw across a chair. "I wasn't expecting anyone to be here." She pulled the robe's collar tighter over her breasts and was satisfied to watch his eyes follow her movements. And more satisfied when they moved down to her hips, and finally to her bare feet.

"I knocked." He raised his eyes to hers again.

"I was in the shower."

"I have a key," he said.

"I know."

"For emergencies and such."

He was flustered. She'd flustered him. *She'd* flustered *him*? It was a powerful feeling to have that effect on a man like Greg McInnis, who, she was sure, could have any woman he wanted. Was he wanting her? Now?

"I'm just leaving Bobby. I thought you might be sleeping." He dropped the damp towel on the kitchen counter, put his hands in his pockets and pulled out a leash and two small cans of dog food and set them on the counter. "How are you this morning, Marcie?"

She pushed a hand through her hair, realizing she hadn't yet brushed it. "Fine, thanks. I slept well. How about you?"

"Fine." Though she didn't think he'd slept well. He looked tired or worried or maybe just preoccupied with some weighty problem.

"I was just about to make tea. Will you join me?" *Please.*

"Thanks, but I want to get to Glasgow as soon as possible." He turned and put a hand on the doorknob. "I'll see you

110

the day after tomorrow. Hopefully, I'll have some answers for you."

Marcie found herself close, drawn unconsciously to him. "Drive carefully."

Greg's eyes searched hers. "If anything comes up you can ring me on my mobile."

She was mesmerized by his eyes, intrigued at how the green deepened as he looked at her. "I'll take good care of Bobby. Be safe and have a good trip." This close his breath warmed her cheek. His size made her feel sheltered. His oiled jacket carried the scent of earth and rain, which she found intoxicating.

"Thanks." He turned to the door, hesitated, then turned back to her. He raised one hand to cup her cheek, then bent to touch his lips to hers, tenderly, yet possessively. "Be careful yourself."

Then he was gone. Marcie stood at the window and watched him cross the small garden and open the gate to the alley. *Be careful.*

***

Greg tried to relax. The Rolls was a pleasure to drive but the memories it evoked of his father pressed in on him. His father had loved the car, had cared for it meticulously, and enjoyed showing it off. Greg couldn't part with it after his father's death, and had taken over its care, care which required taking it out on the road regularly and onto the motorway now and then to run at speed.

Once he was on the motorway, his mind switched to the few minutes he'd just spent with Marcie. She'd looked so alluring dressed only in a scanty robe, her legs long, her feet bare, her hair mussed and damp from her shower. He'd had to curtail those images, but they returned now causing an exquisite tension he had no idea if he'd ever be able to assuage.

He'd wanted to accept her invitation to stay for tea, had even felt compelled to spend the day with her. But he had a job to do. Find Fairmont and light a fire under the man's arse. He hated to see Marcie so worried about her job and about the man who should be in constant contact with her. Fairmont should be helping her along the way, making sure she was not only on schedule but safe and well.

Once in Glasgow, feeling calmer, Greg concentrated on maneuvering through traffic to the offices of Caledon and Bishops.

***

After her tea—during which Marcie hadn't been able to work on her decisions because her mind was filled with churning emotions—she dressed, clipped Bobby's leash onto his collar and walked down the street. A row of shops made up the small, neighborhood business district. Like the houses in the neighborhood, most shops were stucco, some stone and others brick, wall against wall, two and three stories. Some upper floor windows were adorned with window boxes and beautiful lace curtains. The window boxes were spilling over with red geraniums, or hot pink petunias holding their trumpets to the on-again-off-again sunshine. In some, fuchsias hung like delicate oriental lanterns.

Each store had a sign across the front, one red with gilt lettering, another green with yellow letters, and one royal blue with an old English font in white. She itched to paint the buildings, the graphic signs, the solid stonework, the delicate flowers.

She wanted to explore Inverness with Greg as her guide, close by her side, his arm around her shoulder, a welcome weight.

One shop, The Chocolate Cat, tempted her with its displays: shiny bonbons, chocolate truffles, and brightly colored marzipan figurines. She breathed deeply of the rich chocolate aroma then turned and walked away before she lost her willpower to resist.

After returning to Judy's house, she did her exercises with the brace off, then tried to hold a pencil and sketch a fuchsia blossom. It was no good. Disappointment fueled frustration and she took the pencil in her left hand and threw it across the room. *Mustn't rush it. Must follow the therapist's instructions.* She put the brace back on and went to the living room to watch TV.

In a day or two she should be ready to move on. Whether or not she would be able to continue her project, she couldn't stay here much longer. Couldn't continue to take advantage of Judy's hospitality.

***

heR scoccish ceo

Judy came in the back door at one o'clock and almost tripped over Bobby. She reached down to give him a scratch behind the ears. "Hello Bobby, wee pet."

"Are you home for lunch? I've eaten but I can make you something." Marcie went to the refrigerator to pull out makings.

"*Och,* some dimwit in roadworks cut the electrics to our building and the one next door. They said it could take hours to repair, so we decided to take the remainder of the day off. And yes, I've eaten, so you can put that back."

"That's got to be inconvenient. I guess it's good Greg went to Glasgow today. I think he'd be the type to get frustrated with the interruption." If Greg hadn't gone to Glasgow he'd have had half a day free to maybe spend with her. The way he'd kissed her that morning, as though he was sorry to be leaving town, as though he would have preferred to spend the day with her, gave hope to her daydreams.

"Let's go sightseeing." Judy turned on the electric kettle and took down cups for tea.

"What? You and me?"

"Aye. Maybe Anna can join us. Just us lassies. You haven't had a chance to see Inverness, have you? We can go anywhere you want."

"Really?" Marcie got excited. Her dull day brightened. "Then I'd love to go sightseeing. I'd like to do a city tour, then maybe we could go to the Loch Ness monster exhibits? We passed them when Greg took me to the teashop. It looks like fun."

"Aye, we'll do all the touristy things."

"Bobby! I forgot. I have to watch him."

"I've got a corner set up for him in the garage. He's even got his own wee door to the garden. He'll be fine. Now, where else shall we go?"

christy olesen

Small fishing boat docked quayside at low tide

CHAPTER EIGHT

A plaintive whine woke Marcie the following morning. Her room was dark and it wasn't until she looked at the clock that she realized she had overslept. Sightseeing all afternoon, then an evening of pub hopping with Judy and Anna had exhausted her. But, oh, it had been so much fun. She'd spent the afternoon as a tourist and the evening as a local.

Wrapped in her robe she let Bobby out into the back garden and looked at the sky. It was low and heavy, shutting out the morning sun. Once Bobby was in and dried off, she took a shower and dressed in jeans and a T-shirt. She had a long, vacant day before her. But the rest would do her good. She thought about the wonderful day she'd had with Judy and Anna when she should have been concentrating on her options; she hadn't yet set her mind to the decision she needed to make: to stay through July and maybe August, as Judy had suggested, and try to finish her job, or go home as scheduled and try again next year. Was she subconsciously delaying the choice? Hoping someone else would come up with a better option?

The power outage at the office had forced Judy to reschedule some meetings after hours to catch up. She'd told Marcie not to wait dinner for her; they'd likely have something delivered to the office.

Greg wouldn't return from Glasgow until tomorrow morning, so it was Bobby, Rumbles and herself. For the whole day.

The rain started with a deluge that didn't let up until well after lunch. Marcie felt restless. She paced the hall, dusted furniture that didn't need dusting, flipped through magazines she had no intention of reading, tried to plan her future, dared to dream Greg could be part of it.

When the storm passed, she put Bobby on his leash and walked down to the shops. She wandered around not wanting to buy anything, but gave in and purchased some chocolate and then, on impulse, a Scottish folk song CD.

It started to rain again as they walked back to the house. The downpour was too much for her cheap raincoat. It lost its resistance to water and she got soaked. In the house she put the key on the hall table with her purchases and carried Bobby to the kitchen where she wiped his muddy feet, toweled him dry and gave him a biscuit. She settled him on her bed where he curled up next to Rumbles and went to sleep.

She stepped out of her wet clothes and put on her robe. It wasn't warm enough so she borrowed Judy's terry robe she found hanging on a hook in the bathroom.

When she looked through Judy's books, not knowing what she wanted to read, she found a guide to the Isle of Skye. She chose two other books and sat on the sofa, her feet tucked under her.

Flipping through the Skye guidebook dispirited her. Someday she wanted to paint there. The photographs were beautiful, dramatic and captivating. They had to be the work of Greg and Mark. She turned to the back cover. Both photographers were featured with photo and bio. She looked at Greg's photo. He looked so ruggedly handsome, his hair windblown, Skye's wild landscape behind him. That was the Greg she loved. *Loved.* The realization didn't come as a shock. She'd felt it coming on for days, but hadn't allowed herself to own the thought. This love was like nothing she'd experienced before. It was palpable, so real it hurt. Tears stung her eyes but she wasn't going to cry. She was so over that. Instead, she got to her feet and went into her room to do her exercises, got frustrated, tried to take a nap, but couldn't sleep.

For dinner she made tomato soup and a toasted cheese sandwich. She gathered all her watercolors and drawings and carried them and her dinner into the lounge. She put the new CD into Judy's stereo and turned the volume up, then sat cross-legged on the floor. Memories overwhelmed her as she sat with all the images spread about her. She was lucky; she had strong memories of each place, where a tourist might stop, look and take a photo or two then move on, she'd spent an hour or more studying each scene, taking in every detail and putting it on paper.

Frustration at not being able to continue her project plagued her and added to her restlessness. She so wanted to be out painting. She had several good paintings and three pages of small vignettes, which didn't count toward her total. But there was no way she could do all the rest in the few weeks she had left in Scotland. She would not reach her goal. Not this year. Every time she thought of it, she had to force back a deep disappointment. In her situation and in herself.

She studied each image in turn, concentrating on those she'd done when Greg had been with her. The memories were of more than just the scene she had painted. She thought of the things she had learned about him: His love of the outdoors, his loyalty to his friends, his pride in his family's business, his considerate care when she'd most needed someone.

Her dinner grew cold, forgotten.

***

On his way back to Inverness, the Rolls' classic comfort did nothing to ease Greg's tension. He'd lied to Marcie. He'd been lying to her from the first, and every time it was harder to look into her trusting eyes and tell her more lies. The fact that he was trying to protect her didn't help. She was strong; she could handle the truth. But he was compelled to keep her from discovering her dream job no longer existed. He didn't want to cause her that pain, that disappointment. He hoped it could wait until he had something to offer her in its place.

He didn't want her reason for being in Scotland to vanish.

The trip to Glasgow had been a disaster. The Caledon and Bishops offices were about to implode. Half the employees, including Fairmont, had deserted to find jobs elsewhere while those who had stayed struggled to keep the place functioning, none quite believing McInnis House Press would soon own Caledon and Bishops.

He'd been looked at with suspicion and outright dislike. The reception by his acquaintances still there was cool. The afternoon spent meeting with different managers and editors, answering questions and reassuring them, had been risky. He'd jeopardized the entire deal by going there, and if his grandfather found out, Greg would be called to Fort William for a 'conference.' His chances of turning *interim* into *permanent* would vanish. He'd taken a big risk, risked his place in the family business, risked his credibility with Marcie.

Greg had spent the next morning trying to locate Fairmont. When that resulted in no leads he decided to cut his trip short and return to Inverness early.

He was in a fine temper by the time he reached Inverness. But he had to go to Judy's house to pick up Bobby. And see Marcie. She'd been on his mind the entire trip. He'd failed her and didn't know how he would tell her.

***

Marcie was still sitting on the floor, her watercolors surrounding her, singing along with the "Loch Tay Boat Song," a little off tune, when she stopped and without turning around said, "Hi Greg. Come for Bobby?" She turned then to look up at him towering over her. Her heart raced seeing him in the lounge doorway, Bobby wiggling with excitement in his arms. His hair was wind blown. He hadn't shaved. Water drops sparkled on his oiled jacket and he looked like a storm, ready to howl. Probably because she hadn't put the chain on the door. Just the same, she wanted to swallow him whole. But why did he have to come in now? When she looked like something dredged up from the bottom of Loch Ness?

"How did you know it was me?" He stepped into the room and turned down the music.

"I heard Bobby's nails on the floor as he came down the hall headed for the front door."

"You could hear that but not hear me knock?"

She had no answer. She wondered why he was angry.

"The door was unlocked. I could have been an intruder."
His voice was low and gentle but held an edge she hadn't heard
before.

"If you were an intruder Bobby would have made a fuss
and bit your ankle."

"Always lock the door when you're alone."

"It's a nice neighborhood," she said, feeling
argumentative.

"Aye, but it's not far from a not-so-nice neighborhood.
Just do as I say and remember to lock the door."

Just do as I say... humph. "Sure. I thought you were in
Glasgow until tomorrow morning."

"I finished early."

"Did you see Mr. Fairmont? Did he explain why he hasn't
returned my calls?"

"Yes, I saw him. They're doing some restructuring. He
said he'd call soon."

He put Bobby down. The little dog made a beeline for
Marcie's toasted cheese. But he wasn't as quick as his master, who
picked up the plate with the cold soup and half eaten toast. "This
your supper?" He didn't wait for an answer but turned and headed
down the hall. She heard the water run in the kitchen and knew
he'd sent her dinner down the drain.

While he was gone Marcie gathered her paintings into a
neat stack. She had so longed to see him but he was in such a
temper. He must be tired of her and think her a nuisance. Or maybe
his trip to Glasgow hadn't gone well.

He came back into the living room and held out his hand
to her. "Get up, put on your purple dress and we'll get a proper
meal."

She took his hand and stood, didn't want to let go. "I don't
want to go out with you. You're angry about something and ill
tempered. Did you have a bad trip?"

"Aye. Hurry along, I'm famished." He dropped her hand
as though it had become too hot, and stepped back.

"You are? I can fix you something." Concerned for him,
she forgot her peevishness.

"No, we'll go out. Now run along and get dressed." He stood in the hallway opposite her bedroom, and leaned against the wall with his arms crossed. She heard his stomach growl.

After dressing, she passed him on her way to the bathroom. "Still there? Why don't you go sit in the living room?"

"I'm fine."

When she returned from the bathroom, as ready as she could be, he looked at her, frowning.

"I still don't want to go out with you," she said. "You're angry and ill tempered and—"

"And you're not? Have you got something to put over that dress? Wind's up."

"All I have is my raincoat. It got soaked and it looks a mess. It'd look stupid over this dress." Why was he provoking her?

"I'm sure Judy has a cardi you can borrow." He pushed off from the wall.

"Greg! You can't go in there, that's Judy's room!"

"How can someone so organized at work be so disorganized at home?" His voice came muffled from deep within Judy's closet. He came out with a sweater a darker plum than Marcie's dress. "Here, put this on." He held it up for her. "You're not as tall as Judy but you're about the same... er... circumference."

She put her left arm in then, twisted to put in her right. "I can't. My brace will ruin it if I try to put my arm through."

He took the sweater off, turned her to face him, gently removed the brace, slipped her arm into the sleeve then put the brace back on over the sweater. His tender, careful touch belied his stormy mood. It made her want to stop this nonsense with the sweater and wrap her arms around him. She'd missed him so much. But she went along with what he wanted to do.

He helped her pull the sweater all the way on then bent to button it. His face was so close to hers it made her dizzy. His woodsy cologne and the outdoorsy scent of his oiled jacket mixed with the clean fragrance of shampoo to produce a heady temptation to run her fingers into his hair and pull him close.

"This looks stupid." Frustration made her crosser. "Oh, no, it's cashmere! I can't wear this. What will Judy—"

He fastened the last button then raised his head, looked at her with an intensity that disorientated her. She wasn't sure if she moved or he did, maybe they both moved. But they moved in such a way to bring their lips together in a hot, searching kiss. She clung to the damp, stiff fabric of his jacket as she leaned into him, forcing him against the wall. She was so ready to quench the thirst, ease the tension. So ready for his lips on hers.

His strong arms wrapped around her, pressing at the small of her back, then cupping her behind and pulling her tighter against his muscular body. She drew her hand down his whiskered jaw and paused on his corded neck where she felt his rapid pulse. His moan vibrated into her fingers, into her core.

He ended the kiss, leaving a delicious pool of heat in her belly.

"She won't mind," he said, breathless, his voice deep, smooth and a little stunned.

"Who won't mind? About what?" Marcie said, dazed. He looked at her as though he was surprised to find her in his arms, but he didn't let go. Which was a good thing as she thought she would drop to the floor in heap if he did.

"Judy, she won't mind if you wear her... thing."

"Sweater?"

"Aye, her cardi, jumper, whatever. She won't mind." He bent to kiss her again. Then, "Where is she?"

"Who?"

"Judy." He brushed his fingers through her hair, pulling it away from her bruised forehead. He stroked the area with his thumb, then kissed it.

"The office. Late." She tilted her head back as he pressed warm kisses down her cheek, then her neck. She loved the way he cradled her head in one large hand and pulled her close, so close, with the other. It made her feel almost fragile, as if he were afraid he'd break her. It made her feel cherished... adored... one step closer to *loved*.

"Because the power was cut yesterday?" He returned his lips to hers, so that she was unable to answer for a moment.

"Yeah, she'll be home late."

"Let's not go out." His breath was hot on her ear as he dropped a kiss on her neck.

"My thoughts exactly."

He scooped her up in his arms and headed to her bedroom, then stopped in the doorway.

"What's wrong?" she said.

"Can't. Not here, it's Dafe's room." He turned and took a few steps down the hall. "Definitely not here," he said at Judy's bedroom door.

"The living room?" Marcie felt the moment sliding from her grasp and tightened her arm around Greg's neck.

"No drapes." He turned and leaned his back against the wall. He let Marcie slip gently to her feet. "And I'm not prepared."

"Not prepared?" Marcie's brain was having trouble switching gears. She still leaned against him, still had her arm wrapped around his neck, still buzzed.

"I don't have any protection with me. And I'm not sure we should take this further. Not yet, anyway."

"Oh." Disappointed, Marcie slipped her arm down his chest and laid her hand against his heart. It was still beating overtime. "I'm sorry."

"Me, too." He walked to the front door, pulled her close and kissed her once more. A promise. Soon. He scooped up Bobby and let himself out.

As Marcie closed the door she heard him say, "Put the chain on."

***

Friday night she and Greg went out together on a real date, dinner at a restaurant overlooking the canal locks. The days were long, and the low sun intensified the colors of the boats as they progressed from lock to lock, a slow, lazy process.

Neither mentioned the night before, yet there wasn't any awkwardness. In fact, they both seemed to simmer below the surface knowing their time together would come soon. Greg's subtle flirtations stretched Marcie's tension to near breaking point. She wanted him more every moment they were together.

They didn't discuss business, but shared stories of their youth and college experiences. Greg entertained her with more stories about his photography trips with Mark.

122

He picked her up in the Rolls and she began to appreciate the car's roominess and comfort, especially when Greg found a private place to park on the way back to Judy's house.

Saturday Greg picked her up in the Land Rover for that promised walk and they drove east from Inverness to Culloden Moor battlefield. They followed a trail through the rough, windswept grass dotted with dandelions and small wildflowers. Stone slabs sat here and there, their sharp edges weather worn, more boulders than memorials. Clan names had been carved into the stones: Clan Stewart of Appin, Clan Mackintosh, Clan Cameron... The carvings were blurred with time and speckled mosses and lichens. Marcie imagined painting vignettes of the stones scattered on a sheet of watercolor paper. A spatter of alizarin crimson and cobalt blue to give the stones texture, a thin line of French ultramarine to give the carvings depth. A dozen shades of green for the grasses they rested in.

A haunting breeze filtered through the trees, accompanying Greg's low voice as he related the battlefield's history. It was a melancholy place, she decided. But an important place in the Scottish people's history. Greg's history. He took her hand as they walked on.

"Do you have ancestors who fought in the battle? Is there a stone for your clan?" she asked.

"There's no stone with our name on it. It's possible they fought here, though records are hard to trace. My grandfather says McInnis men followed Prince Charlie here, but he's been known to rewrite history to suit himself."

She laughed, then sobered. "It must be comforting to have a long family history. To know where you come from."

"It does give one an anchor to a place."

"I've only met one grandmother, my father's mother. She lived in North Carolina and I spent a couple weeks with her one summer when I was twelve. Colleen Douglas Winters. Her husband, my grandfather, died in World War II and she raised my father alone. She never remarried."

"Douglas is a common surname in Scotland, and Colleen has long been a popular given name. Maybe she was Scottish, or her ancestors were."

Marcie felt a small, tentative connection to the land. She regretted having to leave it so soon.

The trail branched and stopped near some trees. Beyond, a rough field, dark green brush tinged with pink and purple, spread out before them. Thinking she might have ancestors connected to this land and its history gave her an awareness beyond her interest in its natural history, art and architecture.

"The battlefield has been left uncultivated, as it would have been at the time of the battle."

"How could they fight in that? Is it heather?" Marcie stepped into the brush for a closer look.

"Aye. And other heath."

"I've never seen it up close."

Greg pulled out his phone and looked at it. "It's my aunt, I need to take this. Excuse me."

When Greg stepped away to take the call she crouched down to take a closer look at the tiny blossoms growing along the tips of the plants. After a few minutes, he rejoined her.

She ran a spike of flowers through her fingers. The blossoms were damp, yet papery, their detail amazing. "It's beautiful, thousands of little bells. I can almost hear them ringing in the wind. Tiny, tinkling, bells." She drew in a breath and let it out on a sigh of pure pleasure. "It has an unusual fragrance: earth and time and long lost love." They stood and looked out over the moor.

She felt sad. So many men had lost their lives fighting for something so basic as the freedom to govern themselves.

As they toured the visitor center, Greg took another call and Marcie felt him distance himself from her. Was he getting impatient as she read each diorama and studied each exhibit? Had she overstayed her welcome?

In the parking lot, after they left the visitor center, Greg surprised Marcie when he handed her a bag. She pulled out a scarf in a beautiful deep blue and green plaid. She was a little disappointed it wasn't the same plaid as his tartan tie she'd come to associate with their first erotic kiss. Nevertheless, it was a gift he'd chosen for her and she would cherish it.

"I noticed you were cold, this will help" He took it from her, shook it open and laid it across her shoulders.

"Thanks. It's beautiful. So soft and warm."

"It's lamb's wool, the best fiber for our climate."

She pulled it close. It did keep the chill away.

"It's Douglas," he said.

"What?"

"You said your grandmother was a Douglas. This is the Douglas tartan."

"Oh, wow. It is? That's so cool." It meant even more to her now. He'd remembered and he'd bought it for her. Her eyes watered and she blinked away happy tears, then reached up and kissed him.

She climbed in the Land Rover and he buckled her in before closing the door and going around to his side.

"What are we going to do, Greg?" Marcie said when they were on their way. The thought of going home, home to California, haunted her. How could she leave, how could she stay?

"About what?"

"This." She waved her hand between the two of them. "Us. We have something. Where's it going to go? Is it just a summer romance?"

Greg stopped the car on the side of the road and turned off the engine, then turned to her. "I can't give you more than a mentor gives a protégée."

"Protégée? Oh, please. I don't want to be a protégée. Been there, done that. It didn't work out so well."

"I'm sorry, I can't give you more, I don't have it in me."

She didn't believe that, not after the way he'd cared for her, the way he'd kissed her.

"Why do you think that? Did you break someone's heart?" She knew as soon as she'd said it that she'd stepped over an invisible line. His expression turned dark, then blank, showing no emotion at all. She wondered how he did that, because she was sure her growing love for him was obvious. She didn't know how to hide it; she didn't want to hide it.

He stared forward but made no move to start the car or move on.

"I'm sorry. It's none of my business." She fiddled with the fringe on her scarf so she wouldn't have to look at him.

They sat in silence. Marcie looked out at the heather-covered hills and stretches of green farmland, but watched Greg in her peripheral vision. He rested one hand on the steering wheel, his thumb rubbing small circles over the leather, the same way he'd rubbed her neck the night at Marks's, as if deciding what to say. Perhaps he would tell her it was time to move on, to continue her trip, even if she couldn't continue painting.

Then he surprised her.

"Her name was Emma and I never had a chance to break her heart," he said in a quiet voice.

Marcie didn't reply. If he wanted to tell her he would. She wouldn't prompt him. After another long silence, in which Marcie watched a farmer run a combine that turned cut hay into large round bales, Greg spoke again.

"That trip had been the most adventurous, most exciting photographic expedition I'd ever been on, because I had her to share it with. We married on a whim before we started for base camp. She was good for the team, her photographic skills fit in with the rest of us. Mark and Aaron shot the fauna and flora, Jeff and I shot scenics, Emma captured the people. She could capture more soul in the face of a Sherpa than any of us ever could. They seemed to relate to her. They looked into the lens of her camera as if they were looking into the eyes of a kindred soul.

"It was her first major expedition. She was strong and could keep up with the men. But some people, no matter how strong they are or how fit, can't handle high altitude. She developed High Altitude Cerebral Edema. We couldn't evac her because of the blizzard. She died in my arms. I should have insisted on more thorough physicals to be sure everyone on the team could handle the altitude."

Marcie pulled the scarf closer as his words chilled her. "I'm so sorry." If he was warning her not to fall in love with him because he couldn't reciprocate, it was too late.

Greg started the engine and drove Marcie back to Inverness. Neither of them spoke until Greg pulled the car to a stop in front of Judy's house.

"I'm sorry I intruded. It was thoughtless of me. You've done so much for me and I'm very grateful." But he was still troubled; she could see it in the furrow of his brow.

"Don't worry about it." He leaned over and kissed her, a kiss so tender and gentle it contradicted the words he'd spoken earlier. He couldn't love her, but he could make exquisite love to her. Didn't he know the way he made love to her demonstrated his feelings for her? Those feelings, nurtured carefully, could bloom into the real thing.

"I'm sorry if I seemed preoccupied at Culloden," he continued.

"The calls? Is something wrong?" She was sure that was it. The call he'd taken from his aunt when they were standing in the battlefield was the moment he'd withdrawn from her.

"My grandfather is ill."

"Oh Greg, I'm so sorry. You should have said something, we could have left immediately."

He got out, opened her door and unsnapped her belt. "My aunt asked me to come after his tests. He's here in Inverness, so I don't have far to travel. Besides, I'd promised you a day out."

"I enjoyed it. Thanks so much for taking me. And for the scarf. I hope your grandfather recovers soon." She stood in the cottage doorway and watched him return to his car, feeling hopeful.

"Don't forget to lock the door, Marcie," he shouted as he got in the Land Rover.

She watched him drive away, then went into the quiet house, shut the door, turned the bolt and set the chain.

***

"I'm sorry to leave you here by yourself all day," Judy said to Marcie Sunday morning. "I won't be home tonight. It's my parent's fortieth anniversary and I'm sure we'll be partying until late. Tomorrow morning I'll go straight to work from there. You'll be all right?"

"Don't worry about me. Go. Have fun. I'll be fine." Marcie stood at the back door and watched as Judy waved good-bye.

By two she had made oatmeal cookies, cleaned the kitchen and dusted the rest of the house. She'd vacuumed the floors and trimmed the flowers in the window boxes and emailed her friends and family. Then she settled herself in front of the TV to pass the time, but could only think about Greg and his story. No wonder he'd looked heartsore when she'd met him. But the more time she spent with him, the more relaxed and the less troubled he seemed to be. She hoped she'd had a part in easing his pain in the same way he'd helped her.

She waited for her cell phone to ring, hoping Greg would call to let her know how his grandfather was feeling. She'd had such a good weekend she'd put off finding a new place to stay. Judy's son would be home soon and she'd be in the way. After lunch she'd go to the shops, buy a newspaper, and look for inexpensive lodging. Maybe with some distance, she'd be able to wean herself off Greg. It was common sense. After all, she'd be leaving Scotland in less than three weeks. But common sense in the throes of love wasn't one of Marcie's talents.

Curled up on the sofa, Marcie flipped through the channels, resigned to spending Sunday alone. But before she found something to watch there was a knock at the door. She jumped up from the sofa and skipped to the door. With the chain on, because Greg would expect it of her, she opened the door a few inches.

"Mr. Fairmont!"

Lighthouse on Loch Linnhe

CHAPTER NINE

"Let me take the chain off." Marcie was delighted and surprised to see Mr. Fairmont. "Please come in. I'm so relieved you're here." She opened the door wide.

"It's good to see you again, Marcie. I'm glad I found you in. I'm sorry I couldn't let you know I was coming. I called the numbers you sent me. One was wrong and the other kept going to voice mail. Luckily you'd supplied your current address."

"Oh no." Had she messed up Judy's number when she'd emailed it to him? She couldn't remember much about that day except she'd been so scared about not being able to finish her job. "I'm sorry. I lost that cell phone. Then I couldn't get in contact with you."

"That's my fault, and I'll explain momentarily." Mr. Fairmont was a tall, lean man in his late fifties. He had a kind face framed with dark hair, gray at the temples and a dark mustache. His three-piece pinstripe suit, and the briefcase he carried matched Marcie's idea of a stereotypical British businessman. All he needed was a bowler hat and an umbrella tucked under his arm.

Marcie showed him to the living room. "Would you like a cup of tea? I just put the kettle on."

"Yes, thank you. I would." He settled in one of the armchairs next to the sofa and placed his briefcase on the floor beside him.

Presently, Marcie carried in tea and her fresh cookies. She sat on the sofa. "I was worried, Mr. Fairmont." She poured the tea.

"I'm dreadfully sorry about the lack of communication. I have a lot to discuss with you today. Do you have the time?"

"I have all day." She couldn't believe he was here. No word, then suddenly, poof! He was at her doorstep. The relief almost made her giddy.

"Good. A half hour or so should do." He took the cup and saucer she held out for him, then helped himself to two sugars and two cookies. "Um," he said around a crumbly bite. "Excellent. I noticed the delicious aroma when I entered." He sat back and set the cup and saucer on the table beside him. "Let me explain. Caledon and Bishops has been going through a transition. I'll get to that in a minute. But first, I received your email explaining your accident. I was sorry to hear about that. You've been to see the physiotherapist?"

"Yes. He believes I will fully recover." She didn't want to say when until she heard what Mr. Fairmont had to say. She sugared her own tea and sat back. Finally, she would find out what was to happen to her project and her stay in Scotland.

"May I see what you have done since our meeting in Oban?"

"Yes, of course." Marcie brought in her watercolors and handed them to Mr. Fairmont. He settled back in his chair, crossed his legs, and put on reading glasses. He examined each one in turn. Marcie watched his face, anxious for approval. He smiled and even chuckled once or twice. When he came to the last one he went through them again. Then he settled them together and shook his head sadly.

Marcie's heart dropped. "They're not what you wanted?"

"Oh, no. They're excellent. More than I had hoped for. Especially the way you captured the symbols of Scotland in very non-cliché ways: children playing ball with a Scottish terrier, the kilted bagpiper sitting cross legged with the traveling students. Perfect. Your landscapes are exquisite."

"Thanks." Marcie's gratitude at his praise was tempered by his solemn demeanor. Had he guessed that she might not be able to paint as well again?

"I must explain what's happened." Mr. Fairmont handed the watercolors back to Marcie. "I have left Caledon and Bishops." He took off his glasses, folded them and slipped them into his pocket. "Caledon and Bishops is a family-owned publishing house over 130 years old. The last family member interested in publishing has died and another company has moved in and offered to buy it from the heirs. The employees had come up with a scheme to buy the company and this other company pushed us out. I am now redundant and considering early retirement."

Marcie was stunned. What about the book? It took her awhile to unscramble her thoughts. "You don't want to stay with the new company?" she asked.

"That company's principal is someone I could never work for. He is known for his cunning and deceit, an outright liar. But I've said too much. It's a personal matter and does not concern you."

It sure did concern her! What about her artwork? Her licensing agreement? "And the Great Glen Guide?"

"I'm sorry, the project was not far enough along to survive the change in ownership and management."

"I see." Marcie felt as though she stood on shifting sand.

Mr. Fairmont uncrossed his legs and lifted his briefcase to his lap. The snap of the locks jolted Marcie's nerves and she jumped. He pulled out a sheaf of papers, closed his case and set it on the floor again. "I know how much this project meant to you, and I'm sorry it has to end this way. I've made a list of other publishers you might want to contact. They might have use for your images." He handed her the papers. "I know several people at these companies so I've included a letter of introduction to several of them. It's the best I can do."

They sat in silence as Marcie looked at the list and the letters, the words on the pages blurring, making no sense to her at all. Finally she sighed, put them on the coffee table and stood. He stood and picked up his case.

"I'm sorry you've lost your job, Mr. Fairmont. I did enjoy working with you. I've fallen in love with Scotland and I've made some wonderful friends, so all is not lost." She walked him to the front door and opened it. "I hope things work out for you." She held out her left hand and he squeezed it, regret in his kind eyes.

"You're a brilliant artist, I'm sure something will come along soon. Again, I'm sorry this didn't work out. Good-bye, Ms. Winters."

Marcie watched as he walked away, got into an older model silver sedan and drove off, taking with him all her dreams.

***

Marcie paced the hallway chewing on her thumbnail and trying to get her head around what had just happened.

She still had a decision to make. A tough one that would affect her career, the course of her life, even. She wanted to talk to Greg or Judy, ask their advice. But she couldn't bother Judy at her parents' anniversary party, and she hadn't heard how Greg's grandfather was doing. If he was with his grandfather, she wouldn't interrupt him. She decided to call his home phone; if he didn't answer it would mean he was still with his grandfather.

He didn't answer. She waited for the beep.

"Hi Greg, it's Marcie. I hope your grandfather is feeling better. I'm wondering if you have the time, can you call me? I need your advice. Again, I hope your grandfather is well soon."

It looked as if she'd have to make this decision on her own. Which was how it should be. It was her job, her career, and her life.

She had two choices: go to Edinburgh and Glasgow and try to sell what she'd done so far, then propose a project she might not be able to fulfill. Or go home, recuperate and try again. She should probably call her father, but he would tell her to come home to Center City to recuperate.

She didn't want to give up her dream, she wanted to do all she could to make it happen. Only then could she go without regrets.

Marcie decided to walk to the shops and get a newspaper. She'd still have to find a place to move to if she stayed.

She was anxious to talk to Greg, to get his advice she hoped he'd call her back soon. She pulled the cell phone from her pocket and checked that it was on and receiving a strong signal.

She enjoyed walking to the shops. It was a beautiful day, not hot, not cold. Seagulls were complaining in the near distance and a gentle breeze ruffled her hair. Fluffy white clouds moved eastward, slowly today, as though they didn't want to leave Inverness. She didn't want to leave Inverness. She breathed deeply the fresh air. She'd have to leave Inverness if she was to look up publishers on the lists Mr. Fairmont had given her. He hadn't needed to do that, go to all the trouble to make the lists for her and write the introduction letters. She felt sorry for him. He'd lost his job, too.

She looked hard and long at her surroundings as she walked. She wanted to remember this street. She visited each shop and said goodbye to a shopkeeper she had made friends with. At The Chocolate Cat she bought herself some extravagant chocolates as a treat to take on the train to Edinburgh.

She stopped on the sidewalk as a thought suddenly struck her. "Duh! Greg's wanted me to work for his company from the start. Now I'm free to do just that." A man passing looked at her strangely and she smiled back, excited as new possibilities started to unfold before her.

She'd call Greg again, this time on his cell phone. If he didn't want to be disturbed, he'd have it turned off and she'd leave a message. And if his grandfather wasn't too ill, she knew he'd call back as soon as he got the message.

She almost started skipping, she was so excited. Even though she had the cell phone with her, she wanted to call from the house. She stopped just long enough to pick up a copy of the *Inverness Courier,* then headed back to Judy's house.

As she settled on the sofa to call Greg, a headline on the front page of the newspaper caught her eye. She picked it up from the coffee table where she'd dropped it and read the article.

McInnis House Press buys out Glasgow publisher.
McInnis House Press (MHP) of Fort William and Inverness, Scottish travel guide and nonfiction publishers, has successfully

completed negotiations to purchase Glasgow
based Caledon and Bishops, publishers of
art books and nonfiction.
"It's been a long negotiation, but in the
end Caledon and Bishops has agreed to the
terms. It's a win-win situation for both
parties," said Gregor McInnis, MHP
publisher.
"It's a step forward for both companies,"
said Rowan Tucker, CEO of the Fort William
branch of MHP.

Marcie was confused. Greg knew she had a contract with
Caledon and Bishops, yet he had never mentioned he was
purchasing the company. Neither had Judy. Perhaps they were
sworn to secrecy. But they should have warned her. As a
contractor with Caledon and Bishops, wasn't she entitled to know
what could affect her contract? They had said they were her
friends. As much as it hurt, she now wondered if they had really
meant it.

Was that why Greg was so interested in her work? Did he
know her contract was now void? Was he planning to swoop in
and gather up the pieces at a cut rate because he knew how
desperately she wanted a licensing contract? A good licensing
contract could be worth millions to both the artist and the licensor.

She was dizzy with questions. If only Greg had told her
what his intentions were. She was experienced enough with men to
know they always wanted something. Unfortunately, they never
seemed to want her, for herself. They wanted her talent as an artist,
or her ability as a cook, or her attentions in their bed. Then there
was Joel, who'd wanted her to boost his own ego.

It hurt to think all Greg had wanted was her art. Hadn't he
wanted her company, at least a little? He seemed to enjoy taking
her out, showing her his world, introducing her to his friends. Not
to mention their times together alone. She'd really thought...

She needed to talk to Greg now. She had so many
questions. If only she knew where his grandfather lived, she could
go there and talk to Greg in person. The best she could do was call.
She picked up the cell phone and hit speed dial one. After several
rings someone answered. Not Greg. An older man, but not Greg's
grandfather, surely? "May I speak to Greg, please?"

"He's busy. May I take a message?" The man sounded impatient, as if he'd only answered the phone to stop the ringing.

"This is Marcie…" She needed to say something that would get Greg's attention so he'd take her call. "I wanted to ask him some questions about the merger."

"Are you with the press?" The man didn't wait for an answer but continued. "I'm Rowan Tucker, CEO of McInnis House Press. What would you like to know?" His voice, his whole manner, had changed, as if he welcomed an opportunity to talk to the press.

"No, Mr. Tucker, I'm not with the press. I was talking to Greg the other day, and he mentioned that McInnis House Press was looking for artists. Can you ask him to call me? He has my number."

"You must be talking about his idea for books illustrated with watercolors. I can tell you right now, that will never happen. Miss… Marcie, did you say? Greg is the pup in this company. He's trying to work his way into the pack but he hasn't learned the business yet. McInnis House uses only photographic illustrations. Always has, always will. It is our trademark."

"I see. Can you still ask him to call me?"

"Of course I will. But I must warn you, Greg is rather undependable. He's used to traveling the world at his own whim. I expect he'll soon get tired of his office job and take off to parts unknown. Take my advice, don't wait around for Greg's project. Like I said, it'll never happen. I'll tell him you called." He ended the call and Marcie just sat there, dumfounded. Her heart sank into her shoes. The little hope she had clung to dissipated like rain on hot asphalt. The happiness she'd felt the last few days turned sour. Had Greg been keeping her close to win her over to a project that wasn't even going to happen? Mr. Tucker wasn't the only one to tell Marcie that McInnis House Press used only photographs. Judy had said the same thing.

She should leave now. The sooner she found a buyer for her illustrations, the sooner she could resurrect her dreams. And the sooner she got away from the distraction that was Greg, the sooner she could fall out of love with him. *Never gonna happen.*

She put all her things into her duffle and shoulder bag, stripped the bed and took the sheets to the washer. Then she sat down and wrote Judy a note. She considered writing a note to Greg but didn't know what she could say. In the end she added a *thank you* to him at the bottom.

After calling a taxi, she went through the house one last time to be sure she hadn't left anything. She gave Rumbles a hug, locked the door to the little house and put the key in the mail slot.

She purchased a train ticket for Edinburgh, boarded, took a window seat, and watched Inverness and the best time of her life disappear behind her.

***

It wasn't until Old Gregor was settled in his own bed the next afternoon, with a nurse and his housekeeper to care for him, that Greg felt he could leave his grandfather. Uncle Rowan had taken Aunt Madeline home to rest after their long night at the hospital, and to pack a bag so she could return and stay with her father.

Greg headed straight for Judy's. Rowan had said to call Marcie but she hadn't answered the phone when he'd called back, neither Judy's phone or the mobile he'd given her. He tried three more times as he drove along the shore of Loch Ness.

His feelings for her were all mixed up. Was she the perfect artist to launch his new ideas for McInnis House Press? Or was he falling for Marcie the woman?

He cared for her. He wanted to protect her from the fallout that was coming with the takeover. He wanted her to realize all that her talent could bring her. He wanted… her. But she would be in Scotland for only a short time, then she would return to the States. Unless he had a confirmed contract for her. That would be the one thing that would make her forsake her damned non-refundable ticket and stay in Scotland.

Would he have time to secure that contract? Would he have time to sort out his feelings for her? Would she want to give up her life in the States to be with him? Would he be willing to do the same for her? How could he? If he were still the free-as-a-bird photographer he'd been just a few years ago, he wouldn't hesitate. But now? When he was fighting for his place in the family business? How could he?

He called her again. No answer, again.

Why didn't Marcie answer his calls? All sorts of scenarios tugged at his mind, taking him places he didn't want to go. He stopped at Judy's cottage and walked to the door, knocked. No answer.

Had she gone out, gotten lost in Inverness and couldn't get home? Had she forgotten to lock the door and was now at the mercy of some crazed intruder? Had she tripped over Rumbles and knocked herself out? All the possibilities left him desperate to be sure she was all right, unharmed.

Why didn't she answered the damn phone?

And why wasn't she answering his insistent knock?

"Marcie! It's Greg. Open the door. Please." He inserted Judy's spare key into the lock and opened the door. The chain wasn't on, which meant she had left the house. Or she'd ignored his advice and hadn't fastened it. "Marcie. It's Greg. Where are you, sweetheart? Are you all right?"

He stopped to look in each room. The lounge was empty, dark. He knocked on the door to Dafe's room. No response. "Marcie?"

The only answer to his call was Rumbles' plaintive meow as he came down the hall, stretched languidly, then wrapped himself around Greg's ankles.

Greg pushed open the bedroom door and was shocked to see the bed stripped and the duvet folded at its foot. All Marcie's things were gone. All trace of her was gone, and Greg felt as if he'd been punched in the gut.

He called Judy on her mobile. "Judy, Marcie's gone."

"Gone? What do you mean? Where are you?"

"I'm at your place. She left a message for me to call her and when she didn't answer my calls I came over. She's gone. All her things as well."

There was silence at the other end. Then a muffled noise that sounded to Greg like a Gaelic swear word he wasn't aware Judy knew. "When did she go? Did she leave a note, a forwarding address?"

"I don't see any note."

"Did she take anything, like the family silver?"

"Judy!"

"Sorry, I'm drunk."

"When will you be home?" Was that desperation he heard in his own voice?

"Not until tomorrow. We've been celebrating. I can't drive home tonight, I can hardly walk. I can't usually let go like this. Dafydd, you know. So I'm taking advantage. Besides, I want to spend more time with my family."

"But… I'm sorry." Just because he was worried didn't mean Marcie couldn't take care of herself and Judy couldn't spend time with her family.

It was Greg's turn to swear. He left the house, locked the door and got in the Land Rover still talking to Judy. "Let me know if she calls you."

"Who?"

"You *are* drunk. If Marcie calls you, let me know."

"Of course. How is Old Gregor?"

"Much better. Tests were negative. It was a low blood sugar thing. He'll be put on a special diet and meal schedule, which will probably just make him more ornery."

"I'm glad to hear it. Relax. I'm sure there's a reasonable explanation why she left."

A reasonable explanation? There was nothing reasonable about Marcie disappearing. Where would she go? Why? Greg started the engine and headed home.

***

Marcie arrived in Edinburgh late that afternoon, tired, hungry and heavy-hearted. She climbed up out of Waverly Station to Princess Street and walked to the information center where she could book a bed and breakfast. The streets were crowded and her duffle dragged heavily on her shoulder. Her arm ached.

It was the high tourist season and there were no vacancies in her price range. Few in any price range. But a cancellation had just been called in from a hotel across the street from the information center. It would tax her budget but comfort and convenience were more important to her at the moment than economy. She still had £100 from the sale of the painting of the Uttly cottage. The £300 Greg had given her was probably the only money she would earn this summer. Not a very good return on her father's investment. She booked something less expensive for the next day and reserved it for the week.

The hotel overlooked Princess Street Gardens and Edinburgh Castle beyond. But Marcie wouldn't look at the sights or the shops. She'd drop her stuff in her room, have something to eat, then go to bed.

In her room, physically and emotionally exhausted, Marcie fell back across the huge bed. Amidst the luxurious surroundings she noticed a crack in the otherwise pristine ceiling. "That's me: plain, boring plaster with a crack." Then more optimistically, "But the crack will mend and the color will return." She closed her eyes for a moment and allowed herself to relax.

Hunger made her stir and she was surprised to see she'd slept several hours. Hoping she wasn't too late for dinner, she went downstairs to the restaurant.

She lingered over her dinner, not wanting to return to her room where she would only think about Greg, and watch all her dreams and fantasies fade with the sunset.

Once she was busy following up the lists Mr. Fairmont had given her it would be easier to forget Greg. She'd started this trip without him, she could finish it without him.

***

Monday morning Greg arrived at the office at the same time as Judy. Late. Neither looked ready to face a day's work. She unlocked the door and put her briefcase on the desk before she followed Greg into his office. "You look knackered. Were you out all night?"

"You look a bit peeked yourself. Did you have a good time at your folks?"

"Yes. It was brilliant. Sorry I'm late. I forgot to put my briefcase in the car before I went to my parents' house yesterday. I had to go by home and pick it up. You didn't answer my question."

"I went back to Grandfather's." He hadn't wanted to return to his quiet, dark house. "He had a difficult night, and I stayed to help Aunt Madeline."

"I'm sorry. I'll bring you some coffee."

"Tea."

"Aye, tea. Scones? Marcie…uh… baked them."

"Digestibles, the chocolate-covered biscuits if you have them. Thanks." He knew he was being ornery, but he didn't want any more reminders that Marcie had left without saying goodbye.

He dropped into his chair, picked up a galley and red pen. After staring mindlessly at the page for a few minutes, unable to think of anything else but Marcie, he sat back and turned in his chair to face the window. The clouds were light and feathery and allowed the bright morning sun to pick out the mellow gold stone and red brick of the old buildings across the street.

He threw his feet onto the credenza beneath the window, crossed them at the ankles and sighed. He'd been dumbstruck when he'd found Marcie gone, so suddenly. He hadn't realized she was that independent. He thought she had grown to rely on him, that she needed him. It had felt good to be needed. He'd left Judy's wondering how he would ever find Marcie again.

Greg turned to his computer and opened his email program.

>   Marcie,
>   Why did you leave so suddenly? Are you
>   all right? Is there anything I can do?

He paused, held down the backspace key and started over.

>   Marcie,
>   I was sorry to miss you at Judy's
>   yesterday. I'm sorry you felt you had to
>   leave without saying good-bye.

He paused again, then deleted the email without sending it. What could he say? He turned to the window again. He was tired and weary and worried.

It took Judy longer to get the tea than if he'd wanted coffee. He'd heard her leave the office and guessed she'd had to go upstairs to the kitchen to find some tea and a box of chocolate covered Digestibles. It made him feel like a cad, letting her fetch for him. Yet he didn't move when she came back in with the tray, sat with his back to her, his feet on the credenza, twiddling the pen between two fingers. "If I'd known you were out of tea, I would have taken coffee. I don't mean for you to wait on me."

"No problem. I have news for you and I wanted you to be comfortable before I gave it to you."

He dropped his feet and spun around to face her. "Marcie? Why didn't you say so before? Did she call?"

"I think I know why she left." Judy held out a newspaper, folded to an article.

He hesitated, staring at it, then grabbed it from her hand. "What's this?"

"Friday's *Courier*. I found it this morning when I went home for my briefcase. Marcie must have left it behind."

"How'd this get out? If Grandfather called the press I'll…" He sank back and read the article. "'A win-win situation,' he says. That's a laugh." He sighed. Marcie now knew he'd been lying to her. They'd all lied by omission. No wonder she'd bolted. "Did you find a note?"

"Aye."

"Read it to me?"

Judy pulled a small piece of paper from her pocket and unfolded it. "She says, 'Dear Judy, I'm sorry I have to leave without seeing you again. I must. I want to thank you for all the help and hospitality you have shown me, a stranger. I will always remember my stay with you and Rumbles at Heather Cottage.' Then at the bottom she's added: 'Greg, you have done so much for me, I will always be grateful.' That's all she wrote. She left £100. And this." Judy handed Greg the mobile phone he'd given Marcie. She held out the money and the note, too. Greg took the note. The childish, left-handed writing pulled something tight across his heart. He had to find her. He had to explain.

***

Marcie woke to bright sunlight edging through a narrow opening in the drapes. She pulled them open and consumed the breathtaking view. Over the still dark treetops, rising above the city on its monument of volcanic stone, Edinburgh Castle glowed in the early morning light. Its gray stones reflected the warmth of the sun in royal style. The silhouette of Old Town trailed after it, along the ridge, like the tail of brilliant comet.

Determination filled her with purpose. She would enjoy the day in Edinburgh, explore the city, see as much as she could in one day, learn her way around. No more pity parties like last night. She was over that. Well, no, she'd never get over Greg's lies. But she would pack that hurt away in a corner of her heart where the

141

sun didn't reached, until the memory freeze-dried and blew away like the faded petals of a spent rose on a dry Nevada wind.

After breakfast she checked her luggage in a locker at the train station, then found a stop for the city tour bus. She could get off and on wherever she wanted for one all-day ticket. Just her kind of bargain.

She was excited.

Thrilled to have a day of sightseeing on her own.

Yeah, right.

No, really, she was.

By four o'clock she had traded excitement for exhaustion. Her feet hurt, her arm hurt and her heart hurt. Her heartbreak had trailed behind her all day like a stray puppy begging for attention.

She stopped to listen to a bagpiper serenading tourists at Waverly Station. How was he able to put so many of her emotions into his lament?

Tuckered out in Princess Street Gardens, she sat and rested and hit the preview button on her camera, then scrolled back to examine the pictures she had taken that day: old stone buildings; more overflowing window boxes; the bright red-painted woodwork of a restaurant on the Royal Mile; chimney pots in a row at the top of slate roofs; children playing in the pedestrian, cobblestone streets, Edinburgh Castle and Holyrood Palace.

She came to her photo of the Grayfriars Bobby monument, which reminded her of Greg and his wee Bobby. A part of that deep, frozen corner of her heart cracked.

She scrolled back to the day at Culloden and a photo she'd taken of Greg at the Memorial Cairn. He was so small next to the massive, twenty foot rock tower. Zooming in just distorted the image. She felt she had lost something dear. If only she had other pictures of Greg.

Maybe she should have talked to Greg one last time, given him a chance to explain, asked him outright what his intentions were. He seemed to sincerely want to help her. Then Mr. Fairmont's words came back to her: *The head of that company is someone I could never work for. He is known for cunning and deceit. An outright liar. A charmer.*

Is that why Greg had taken her out? To charm her? To make her want to join him in a project that didn't exist and maybe never would? Tomorrow morning she would call the Edinburgh contacts on the lists. If nothing came of that, she'd make some cold calls, see what happened. And she'd work on getting an appointment with Amanda Roth. The watercolors she'd done so far would have to be enough.

***

It seemed to take forever for six o'clock to come around, and Greg was happy to see it. His attention to his job had been sketchy, given that most of the time he was thinking about Marcie, puzzling out why she'd left so suddenly without asking him to explain the article, and wondering how he would persuade his grandfather to accept his ideas about using painted illustrations when his grandfather was ill. A call from Aunt Madeline, that his grandfather was doing much better, relieved his worry that the old man wasn't suffering from something more serious.

He finished the last email on his to-do list and shut down his computer. With his lack of concentration, it wouldn't do any good to work after hours tonight. He picked up his coat and briefcase and walked into Judy's office. "Done for the day?" She always left promptly at half five and seldom took work home with her. But in the last fortnight, while Dafe was away, she'd often lingered after hours.

"I'm going to pick up Dafydd at the airport. Would you like to come with me?" Judy gathered her things, her computer already shut down.

"Yes, I'll even drive so you can give him your undivided attention." It would give him something to do besides facing an empty evening, and it would be great to see Dafe again.

"That's what I love about you, you're so thoughtful." Judy gave him a kiss on the cheek. "Did you drive the Rolls today?"

"Yes, why? Dafe prefers the Land Rover."

"I've always fancied myself chauffeured to the airport in a Roll Royce." With that statement she walked out the door giving a queenly wave.

***

"Uncle Greg! Uncle Greg! I'm home!"

Greg's heart swelled with the welcome Dafe gave him. The boy ran to him, and Greg caught him up, held him high and spun around. "You're getting too big for this. Won't be able to do it much longer."

Dafe giggled. He held his arms out and made the sound all boys know how to make for jet fighters. Greg gave him a gentle landing, thinking that he'd like to come home to his own child's welcome call of "Daddy!" Some day.

He would be a good dad; he'd had a good example in his own father. The right woman, though, would deserve more from him than he might be able to give. He didn't think he could give her the emotional commitment she needed.

Judy caught up to them and Greg took the boy's bag as they walked to the car.

"I'm glad you're driving, Greg. He's really wound up." Judy and her son climbed in the back seat and Greg played chauffeur.

The drive home was one long, excited monologue of Dafe's holiday in Wales with his grandparents. "Grandpa taught me some Welsh words. He says he'll call me each week and teach me more, but I don't know. They put an awful lot of letters in their words and then double them up and slip them in sideways when you're not expecting 'em. Like in my name."

"It's always good to know another language, Dafe. It impresses the lassies." Greg caught Judy's warning expression in the rear view mirror. "And it gives you a connection to your heritage." *Heritage.* He was well on his way to having no one to pass his heritage to. His family stories—as he knew them—would end with him. He had some good stories to pass down, fishing, hunting, camping, traveling the world.

His line of McInnis would end. That slammed into him unexpectedly. His father had been an only son, Greg was an only son. Posterity pretty much depended on him to repopulate the McInnis name, or there would never be another McInnis at the helm of McInnis House Press. Three or four sons would be a good start. Then at least one would want to take over the business from him.

Dafe went on non-stop about his adventure and was still going strong when they reached Judy's house. "I'll pick you up in the morning," Greg offered, since Judy's car was still in the parking garage at the office.

"Come in for dinner, Greg. I made it yesterday. It'll just take a minute to heat up."

"Thanks, I will." He joined Judy and Dafydd and ended up staying the evening until Dafe unwound enough to fall asleep. The cottage seemed different without Marcie there to greet him. He half expected her to come around a corner, her smile radiating happiness. Even after her accident and the trauma it had caused her physically and emotionally, she still had an optimistic view of life. He caught her perfume lingering here and there in the house, especially when he went into his Dafe's bedroom to see the treasures he'd brought back from Trefriw.

He sat with Judy another half hour, avoiding her searching questions, before he reluctantly left to return to his dark house.

christy olesen

Highland cow

CHAPTER TEN

By Monday evening Marcie had moved from the expensive hotel and stood in her new room at a bed and breakfast in an old, refurbished rowhouse. It was a small room. She had been lucky to find a single at a price she felt she could afford. But she'd saved so much of her budgeted funds staying at Judy's she wasn't too worried about it. It was a nice, quiet neighborhood not far from the town center, where she'd pounded the pavement all day.

She's also found a physical therapist willing to help her and bill her insurance. She would start the next day.

Settled in, Marcie stepped away from the window, went to the small desk and sat. She needed to plan her attack for the next day. With her lists and her city map she marked the places she would visit. When that was done she went to the guest lounge to watch TV and hopefully take her mind off Greg.

***

It was the longest day of the year. Greg remembered how Marcie had wanted to watch the late sunset and wondered if she was somewhere where she could do that. Wherever she was, he wanted to be there with her. The sunset didn't matter to him; he'd seen the midnight sun at the Arctic Circle. But watching it with her, anywhere, would be contentment.

By Thursday, Greg felt he'd finally gotten some work done. His desk phone buzzed. "Are you busy?" Judy asked.

"I'm always busy." Three days had passed since Marcie had left. He'd tried to concentrate on his work, but it seemed he could never catch up. He'd lost his edge, nearly lost his interest. The excitement he'd experienced with his new project and Marcie's importance in its success dissipated with each day she was gone.

He'd composed a dozen emails to Marcie but hadn't sent any. How could he explain to her why he'd lied? How could he make her believe he wanted the best for her? He needed to speak to her in person.

"Can you come out here? I just got an email from MerciMe."

Marcie! Greg's chair squeaked as he pushed away from his desk. He opened the door separating their offices, stood in the doorway and leaned against the jam, arms crossed. "And...?"

"Shall I read it to you?"

"Aye."

```
Hello Judy,
    I want to apologize for leaving so
suddenly. I hated to leave without saying
goodbye. I don't want you to think I don't
appreciate all you've done for me. I do! I
can't explain why I left. Maybe another time
I will be able to tell you.
    Your friend, Marcie
```

Judy turned from the monitor back to Greg. "Should I tell her we know why she left? If I can explain about the takeover maybe she will forgive us and let us know where she is."

"Aye, tell her anything you want." Maybe Judy explaining to Marcie would be a better idea. Or was he just being a coward?

"She's probably still online. Do you want me to call you if she answers?"

"Yes. Please."

***

In an Internet café in Edinburgh, Marcie read Judy's email.

> ```
> Marcie,
>     Hello! I'm so glad to hear from you.
> Where are you? How are you? We've missed you.
> I don't blame you for leaving. I think I know
> why. I found the newspaper you left behind.
> I'm sorry we couldn't tell you about the
> transaction. Legally, we were not allowed to
> discuss it with anyone outside MHP,
> especially anyone affiliated with C&B. They
> have a talented staff. We didn't want any of
> them to leave until we could tell them what
> MHP's plans are. MHP has no plans to dissolve
> the company. We have plans to expand it.
> Unfortunately, as usually happens, word
> leaked out and several of their key people
> have left.
>     I hope this explains things. I wouldn't
> want you to leave thinking badly of us.
>     Your friend, Judy
> ```

Marcie was more confused than ever. She didn't know whom to believe. Mr. Fairmont had said Greg was devious and cunning. Mr. Fairmont had felt so strongly about the buyout of the company he'd worked for for twenty-five years, that he'd left rather than work for them.

Mr. Fairmont had been the first to see her art and see its potential and he had always treated her fairly and courteously. On the other hand, Greg had been there when she'd needed him. In fact, he'd gone out of his way to help her when Mr. Fairmont hadn't returned her calls.

She tried not to let the detail that she loved Greg influence her assessment of him as a businessman. *Right, like* that's *possible.*

She hadn't gotten anywhere yet with the publishers on Mr. Fairmont's lists. What had once been a done deal now looked more like a dream ready to fizzle.

She put off replying to Judy, needing to think about what to say and how much to give away. She thought about emailing her father, but he'd just say I told you so, and tell her to come home and apply for the art teacher job at the Center City middle school.

Feeling pressured by other customers around her, Marcie logged off and left the café. She walked along the street looking in the shop windows absent-mindedly.

She puzzled over what to do next. She felt she had no one to confide in. She couldn't tell her father, he would demand she cut her losses and come home now. Wallie was too busy as an intern for Marcie to feel comfortable bothering her again. Joel was history. Her mom didn't understand why Marcie was there at all.

She walked to Princess Gardens and watched the families on the carrousel, and thought about how to answer Judy's email.

***

Monday morning, a week after Marcie had left, Greg entered the outer office. He dropped his things on a side table and walked across the room to where the photo of Emma hung. He hadn't wanted Judy to hang it at all two years ago, but also hadn't wanted to face her questions so he'd suggested a place out of his direct line of sight when he entered or left their offices.

He had a dream this morning. Emma standing in his room but he couldn't see her clearly. He couldn't remember exactly what she looked like. But he could see a tear streak her cheek just before she turned away and vanished.

Now he looked at the photograph of Emma purposely. It was a compelling photograph, shot at base camp before the storm. Her cheeks were rosy with good health, good spirits and frosty air. Her eyes sparkled as she looked directly at him through the lens of his camera. She looked different. In hindsight he could now see the apprehension in her expression. The restlessness that had pushed her to take risks, the edginess that had made it hard to know her fully. He understood her better after her death than he ever had in the short time they were lovers. Sometimes she sought solitude, shutting him out. When she was like that it was almost as if they were strangers. Other times she couldn't get close enough to him. At the time he'd thought it was being on the expedition. That she wasn't as sure of her abilities as she had made out to be. It made her more endearing to him. He watched after her without hovering, he protected her without it seeming so.

He loved her, but felt the love fading. He missed her from a part so deep within it made him feel hollow. But that was fading, too. Mixed into those gut feelings was an anger he seldom acknowledged. She hadn't told him the complete truth of why she was so eager to join the expedition, why she'd campaigned so hard to be included.

"Greg?"

Startled, Greg turned to see Judy standing close. He'd been so lost in thought he hadn't heard her enter the room. He saw the concern on her face but didn't comment. Instead he turned back to the image of Emma. Something was pulling him to her, something was pushing him away.

"Greg, why are you standing here staring at that picture? You've ignored it for two years. You look upset?"

Still facing the painting, images of the day after the photo had been taken filling his mind. "Today is the day she died. Did you know that?"

"I hadn't thought about it. Two years ago today?"

"I will always remember that day. Did you know she died in my arms?"

"Someone mentioned it. You must have felt helpless. I'm sorry it happened, so sorry."

Greg sighed, then the story tumbled out. "We were married." He ignored her gasp and went on. "For two weeks. An itinerant American preacher in Nepal married us. It was exciting. We felt like kids getting away with something. It was our secret, we didn't even tell the others on the expedition. They probably thought we were having a summer affair." They both moved to the guest chairs against the wall. Greg sat back with his legs stretched out, crossed at the ankle. Judy sat upright, her hands folded in her lap. "I wasn't certain the marriage was legal and promised her a proper wedding when we returned home. She didn't want one. To her, the ceremony in Nepal was all she needed."

"Oh, Greg. Why didn't you tell me before now? I could have helped you."

"You were a great help, empathetic. I shared more with you than anyone else. But I never found a time when I could talk about the marriage. Until now."

"It's part of the healing process. She'll always be with you, but in time the heartache and the anger will dim."

"I didn't say I was angry at her." He was surprised that she had touched what he had just been feeling.

"Anger is part of the process we go through after losing a loved one. Anger that they weren't more careful, anger that they didn't go to the doctor soon enough, or didn't wear their helmet. Anger that they left us behind."

"A few weeks after the team returned home I received a report from the coroner's office. Emma had a congenital heart condition. And she knew about it. Knowing that, I could look back and I think she had wanted to go on that expedition as a last shot at life. During the trip she often said things like, 'This is the life,' or 'Isn't this living?' She had a zest for the adventure. I think she went there to test her endurance. Or to die on that mountain."

"She must have been a special person to endure the hardships of that trip. You know, being able to talk about it now shows you are healing. Do you feel ready to start the rest of your life?"

"Do you?" he asked. She'd lost her husband almost three years ago. Was she ready to move on?

Judy looked down at her hands clutched so tightly the skin blanched and unclenched them, then smoothed her skirt. "Some days I feel like I'm stagnating, that I need to get on with my life. But there are still times when I can barely function." She turned to Greg and touched his arm. "Greg, if you're ready to move on, don't let this opportunity slip by."

Now he was confused. "What opportunity?"

"Marcie." She got up and started making coffee. Greg sat awhile. Was Marcie the reason Emma was fading from his heart. Or was it just time that was pulling her away from him?

Judy put a tray with coffee and scones on Greg's desk. "I've gotten another email from Marcie." He picked up the mug, followed her into her office and stood behind her as she read it to him. Maybe there would be a clue he could use to locate her.

        Dear Judy,
        Thank you for the explanation. It helps
    me to understand what has happened. I am

well. I access my email from an Internet café
a few blocks from where I'm staying. It's a
busy place so I can't stay on line for long.
Please don't think I'm ignoring you.

I'm seeing a very good therapist who's
helped me so much. I am able to do some basic
drawing exercises. I feel I will be able to
draw and paint sooner than I expected.

Did Dafydd enjoy his visit with his
grandparents? I bet you're happy to have him
home. I'm sorry I didn't get a chance to meet
him. How is Rumbles? Do you see Bobby much? I
miss them both. There are no pets where I am
staying.

MW

Hearing from Marcie, even secondhand, only confirmed to
Greg that he wanted to find her. To explain himself. Not make
excuses, but just let her know he hadn't intended to do her any
harm. He didn't want to leave things all unraveled between them.

Judy turned from the computer to face Greg. "She doesn't
give a clue where she is, or even if she's still in Scotland. She
sounds lonely."

"She could be anywhere, emails have no postmark." It
wasn't lost on him that Marcie had asked after Bobby, not him.

"I'll keep writing. Maybe she'll drop another clue," Judy
said as she turned back to her computer.

Greg returned to his desk. He deserved Marcie's rebuff.
He'd lied to her, hadn't given her any reason to trust him. Still, it
hurt that she had contacted Judy, not him. How could he make it
up to her? How would he find her?

***

In Edinburgh, Marcie opened her email.

Hi Marcie.

We're so glad to hear about your
progress, it's very encouraging.

It took Dafydd two days to unwind. He
had a brilliant holiday in Wales. I'm so glad
to have him home safe and sound. It's hard
not to worry about him when he's away from
me.

chRisty olesen

I agree with you, it's nice to have pets around the house. Rumbles is still a rascal, as usual. I often find him wandering the hall looking for you. *He misses you. He's grouchy and short tempered.* ;)

Bobby is as sweet as ever.

Are you still in Scotland? Wish you could have come to Anna McLoud's engagement party. I've attached some photos. Isn't her fiancé distinguished? Greg hosted the party at his home. Anna wants to invite you to their wedding a fortnight from Saturday next. It was a whirlwind courtship!

BTW, Greg wants you to contact him.

Stay in touch, Judy

When Marcie read the email she felt a sudden and intense loneliness engulf her. She'd never felt so lonely before, nor could she define the feeling. All she knew was that it was linked to Greg. With him she'd felt at home for the first time since her parents' divorce.

She loved him. The fact that he'd lied to her broke her heart. Was all his careful attention just his way of gaining her trust so he could acquire rights to her illustrations even though his family wouldn't agree to his project? She felt sorry for him. Evidently, he really wanted to produce the illustrated books but had no support.

The photos Judy had attached were wonderful. One was a picture of Judy and Anna on either side of Greg, his long, muscular arms around their shoulders, pulling them close, his smile not quite reaching his eyes. Was he missing her? Did her care for her at all? To him she was probably just that strange American illustrator who had fallen at his feet when he wasn't looking. He'd almost certainly forgotten her by now, had probably forgotten what she looked like; she had that kind of face.

***

Greg remembered Marcie. It wasn't hard. He missed her open trust and friendliness, her compassion for others. He missed her big blue eyes, expressive, betraying her feelings; her smile, given freely and unselfconsciously, lighting her face; her figure, soft and curvy, long and slender.

154

What could he do to regain her trust?

He pulled his camera from the bottom desk drawer and turned it on. He wanted to see Marcie. *No Images.* The message on the screen reminded him that he'd given the memory card to Mark. He always backed up his photos on the company server so he put the camera away and turned to his computer. Then he remembered. He'd downloaded the card before he'd met Marcie at Loch Leven. The only photos he had of her were in Mark's possession. Frustration agitated him.

"Greg, another message from MerciMe."

He went to the open doorway and waited for Judy to open the email and read it aloud.

> Dear Judy,
> I would like to attend Anna's wedding, but I can't promise I will be able to. Thank you also for the photos. You all look so happy. I guess I missed a great party.
> Judy, please don't share the rest of this message with…

Judy's voice petered out. She stopped and turned to Greg. "Sorry."

"I get the hint, girl stuff." He went back to his desk and wondered how he might hack into Judy's email to read the message, then wondered how he had come to such a state.

Restless, he returned to Judy's office. "What's she say? Any clues to her whereabouts?"

"She's safe, that's all."

"But she told you where she is? That's why you're red in the face. Don't you know a ginger lass canna lie?"

"I'm not lying. She asked me not to tell…"

"Not to tell me? I see… But she's all right? She doesn't need anything? Money? Shelter? Friends?"

"She's fine." Judy turned back to her computer; the email message was still up on the monitor. She scrambled to close it.

"Never mind. I have good eyesight. She's in Edinburgh."

Greg wasn't surprised at the enormous relief he felt, finally knowing where Marcie was. She'd been in his thoughts since she'd left Judy's house. Since he'd met her, if he were honest with himself.

He walked past the printer and noticed photo paper in the tray. "Is this the Alaska cover mockup?" He picked up the glossy paper and turned it over. Marcie. Her smiling face made his chest tighten. God, she was beautiful! He hadn't realized before just how beautiful she was.

"It's just a few pictures Anna took when we went on the city tour."

Judy's cheeks were still flushed and he guessed she'd printed out the photos for him to find. "When was that?"

"When you were in Glasgow. The day they cut the electrics. Anna and I showed Marcie the town and Loch Ness. You can have those."

"You had a good time."

"Aye, we did. Marcie's great fun, especially when she's not worried about her future. She has a brilliant sense of the absurd. Do you know where she wanted to go more than anywhere else?"

"The monster exhibits?" It wasn't hard to guess looking at the pictures. In one Judy and Marcie were posing near the Nessie sculpture on the exhibit grounds. They were both laughing, Marcie's face radiant with good fun. He had never seen her quite like that and he felt he'd missed something special. "Anna should go into outdoor portrait work. These at Urquhart are very expressive."

Anna had caught Marcie as she leaned over a ruined wall at Urquhart Castle gazing at Loch Ness with an expression of awe and wonder. And fear? She looked as though she were afraid, yet fascinated, to look over the ruined wall to the loch below.

Judy stood and looked at the photos with him. "Strange thing. She says she's afraid of heights, but never was before her accident. You'd think she'd gain a fear of driving, or something related to the accident."

"But she climbed to the top of the Urquhart tower and is looking over the drop off." He wished he'd been there to make her feel safe. He would have held her hand as they climbed the steps of the ruined tower, he would have held her close and circled her with his arms as they looked over the wall to the deep, dark water below.

"She loved Urquhart." Judy said. "She wants to paint there someday."

"She will." He wanted to be the one to take her there, and so many other places he knew she'd love.

The next photo must have been taken a moment later as Marcie looked at the camera and blushed at being caught unaware. A delicate smile touched her lips. A *Mona Lisa* smile.

Greg needed to make some phone calls. His network of friends in the business was vast, he started calling contacts in Edinburgh.

When he finished his calls he buzzed Judy. "Can you clear my calendar for tomorrow?"

"No way, boss. It's the big post-transaction meeting at nine at Mòirneas . It will probably last all day."

"Right. How could I forget?" Not knowing where Marcie was, how she was, was interfering with his concentration. He needed to find her. "How about Wednesday?"

"Two meetings with editorial and one with production," Judy reminded him.

"But nothing urgent."

"No, I can move them. But we should keep the day open if the post-transaction isn't finished up."

"That's not likely. Grandfather will want it all wrapped up with a bow before tea. I asked Rowan to talk to him about postponing because of this setback with his health, but Granddad's a stubborn old coot."

"What will I say? When I move the meetings, I mean?"

"Say I'm going out of town."

"Where?" she asked.

Greg paused. "I suppose I have to tell you."

"I'll find out anyway."

"Aye, you will, too. Edinburgh."

christy olesen

Memorial Clan stones at Culloden Muir battlefield

CHAPTER ELEVEN

Greg wasn't sure how he'd gotten through the all-day, post-transaction meetings. Auto pilot, maybe. Part of his brain had paid attention to and participated in the proceedings; the other part had planned how he would find Marcie.

His grandfather's health had improved and the old man had managed to preside over the meetings like a statesman.

The next morning Greg was in Edinburgh, driving through traffic, following GPS directions to the first Internet café on his short list. Checking Internet cafés was the only thing he could think of. She was in one almost every day, emailing Judy and most likely her friends and family. Whoever worked there might recognize her. Then he'd narrow his search.

He had one day to find Marcie. The calls he'd made had worked. Two of his contacts had received calls from Marcie Winters, one of whom had set an appointment for her to come in. Unfortunately, that appointment had taken place the day before his call. Another contact had a cold call from her and had asked her to come back in two days. If Greg couldn't find her today, he'd come

back and intercept her at her appointment. He could just imagine
Marcie going from publisher to publisher, trying to sell her
illustrations. A real trooper. A desperate trooper.

Greg had to admit that Marcie might be impossible to find.
What right did he have to interfere anyway? She was under no
obligation to him. She had been happy with her contract with
Caledon and Bishops. Then he had come onto the scene and taken
that away from her. Actually, his grandfather had taken it, but
Greg felt as responsible. Now Marcie was on her own, looking for
another publisher, hanging on to her dream. He had nothing
concrete to offer her, yet right now he was feeling cavemanish
enough to drag her back to Inverness with promises he wasn't sure
he could keep.

Greg's GPS got him to the general vicinity of the first
Internet café but he couldn't see it. He parked and started
searching on foot. After having no luck he stopped a young man on
the street. "Do you know where the Internet café is?"

"Aye, just around the corner. But they don't open until
three."

"Thanks." Greg stood with his hands on his hips. It
couldn't be that one because Marcie had emailed Judy in the
morning.

"There's access at the library," the young man said
helpfully.

Again, Greg thanked him, then got in his car. Marcie had
specifically said Internet café. Not the library or hotel lobby or any
other venue.

Greg looked for and found the next one on his list but had
to park two blocks away.

About halfway there he pulled out his mobile phone and
called the office. "Judy, have you had any messages from Marcie
this morning?"

"Where are you?"

"I'm on my way to an Internet café in New Town to see if
anyone there has seen her."

"Brilliant. She's online now. I don't know how long she'll
stay. Get there quick!"

Greg put his phone back in his pocket and started to jog,
weaving around morning pedestrians on their way to the coffee

stands, news agents or bus stops. He was so close, he had to find her. What he'd say or do when he did, he wasn't sure.

He reached the Internet café and stopped at the open door. As he caught his breath he looked around and saw Marcie sitting at a corner kiosk with her back to him. The relief he felt at seeing her again was so keen he was afraid he was only seeing what he wanted to see, afraid she'd disappear like an image on a monitor when the power is cut. He walked up behind her and stopped. It took all his will power to keep his hands off her. She lifted her right hand to tuck a stray lock of hair behind her ear. He noticed she wore a smaller brace and typed hesitatingly with that hand. Her injury was uncovered and except for some lingering redness around a jagged scar, it looked to be healed.

Both her hands paused above the keyboard and she said without turning around, "Hello Greg. Come looking for me?"

She turned then to look up at him. He watched various emotions cross her face: surprise, delight, consternation. He felt the same emotions race through himself.

"How do you do that? How did you know it was me?"

"I'm psychic? I could say I sensed you because we have a connection. But that would be a *lie*, wouldn't it? I saw your reflection on the monitor."

"Are you writing to Judy? Tell her I'm here and log off."

"I'm not finished."

"Do as I ask, Marcie." *Please.* He didn't know how long he could hold out before he pulled her into his arms.

She looked up at him, rolled her eyes, then turned back to the computer with a flourish that caused her hair to spin like a dancer's skirt. "When I'm finished."

He stood, he waited, he fretted. But he no longer pushed. Who was he to tell her what to do, even make a request? Just because he was so relieved to find her didn't give him the right to demand she come with him.

When she finished, she stood and led the way out. "Where are we going?"

"Somewhere to talk. But first…" He pulled her into the shadowed doorway of a closed shop, bent and kissed her. He meant to be quick about it, to prove something to himself. But his will power gave in to his desire and he lingered. He pulled her close and lost himself in her softness, her warmth, buried his fingers in the silk of her hair, cupped his hand on the firm roundness of her bottom.

And he proved two things:

One, he wanted her; his body wanted her.

Two, she didn't seem to want him.

She hadn't resisted, but unlike their other kisses, she hadn't responded either. Not in that uninhibited, enthusiastic way that had drilled him to the core. The memory of that had disturbed his nights ever since their first kiss. But this—not reacting at all—was new territory for him. Women usually responded positively, passionately, to his kisses. Marcie threw him off balance, and she had done so since he'd first met her. "Marcie?" He let his arms fall from her.

"Why are you here?"

"I'm not sure. I guess I had to be certain you were all right. You disappeared and we were worried about you."

"I'm okay. I told Judy I was okay."

He leaned his head back against the shop door. "I'm sorry. I was... I shouldn't have..."

"Is the big publisher at a loss for words? Let's call the press." Her sarcasm didn't quite reach her eyes; in fact, he saw mischief dancing in their blueness, and it gave him hope.

"It's you who make me speechless, Marcie."

"You're right, we need to talk." She stepped back onto the sidewalk. "You're acting strange. I'm not sure if I'm glad to see you."

"First, I want to say I'm sorry you were a victim of my family's business ventures."

"Oo, fancy talk. But thanks." She smiled half-heartedly.

***

When they reached his Land Rover, Marcie let herself in as soon as he popped the locks. She fastened her seat belt and sat with her hands in her lap, still trying her hardest to suppress the joy she'd felt since seeing his reflection in the monitor at the Internet café.

Good thing Judy had warned her that Greg was on his way. It had given her time to compose herself. She thought it would be best not to show any emotions until she understood what he wanted. It was the most difficult thing she'd ever tried to do.

"I'm glad to see your hand has improved." Greg clicked his own belt into place.

"It has, quite a bit. Where are we going?"

"We're going to get some breakfast."

"I've had breakfast," she said.

"So have I. Hours ago. Can you suggest someplace?"

"The Internet café?"

He looked at her, then smiled, just the way she loved to see him smile, with no reservations. "I meant a real breakfast."

"Turn left, two blocks, then left again and halfway down the street."

Once inside the restaurant, they found a table by the window. Marcie sat and took in the old but well cared for interior. A bit of morning sun made the cut glass condiment holders on the table look like exquisite crystal. Tiny flashes of rainbow refracted onto the white linen table cloth and sparkled on the chrome toast holder. A fresh rosebud in a glass vase echoed the pink rose wallpaper. The high ceiling was trimmed in white crown molding and the tall casement windows were framed with green velvet drapes. It was cozy and elegant. She'd passed it a few time in the last week, but had never entered. It looked expensive.

"What would you like?" Greg asked.

"An English breakfast with bangers."

Greg ordered the same, then turned to her when the waitress left. "I'm so sorry your contract was canceled. I feel responsible, since it was my family's business that set those events in motion."

"I appreciate the sentiment. It's a hard business to break into and I thought my opportunity had arrived. I'll just have to try harder."

"There are other publishers besides Caledon and Bishops."

She pulled two folded papers from her bag and laid them on the table between them, pressing out the creases with her hand. "Here're two lists of Scottish publishers. Note I have highlighted over twenty possibilities. I've already called on all the ones in Edinburgh. Next, Glasgow."

"Aye." He studied her lists. "You missed one." He pointed to a listing she hadn't highlighted.

"McInnis?"

"Of course. I told you I could help you with licensing."

"Yes, but all the illustrations you publish and license are photographic. Judy told me you use photography *exclusively*."

"True. But there's always room for change."

"When will that change come?"

Their breakfasts arrived and she aimed her fork for the nearest banger, loving the way the skin popped and the juices ran over her fork.

"I wanted to sign you the first day—"

"I remember how insistent you were."

"Then the merger happened before I expected. I didn't know if your contract would survive or not. I didn't want you to worry about that while you were dealing with your injury."

"Still, I would have liked being informed about something that could affect my future. It was quit a shock when Mr. Fairmont—"

"He finally called you?" Greg looked surprised.

"He came to the house. He told me, among other things, that he couldn't work for the company that bought out Caledon and Bishops because the publisher was an out and out liar. I didn't know until later that he was talking about McInnis House Press."

"He was talking about my grandfather," Greg said with resignation but no apology.

"I thought maybe he was talking about you."

"Me? The publisher? Hardly. I'm just—"

"'The pup in the family business'? That's what Mr. Tucker said."

"Mr. Tucker? You mean Rowan Tucker, my uncle? When did you talk to him?"

"When I called you that Sunday, when you were at your grandfather's, he answered your phone. I didn't know he was your uncle."

"What else did he say?"

Marcie hesitated, but if she wanted to get everything out in the open between them, she'd have to do her part as well. "He said that McInnis House Press would never use anything but photographic illustration. He said I shouldn't count on you since you would soon tire of your office job and go back to being a free lance photographer."

"Not true, the part about my leaving my office job. It's part of who I am. It's my inheritance from my father. As far as my idea of using your watercolors, I have to convince Rowan and Granddad—"

"Which is pretty much e-talk for *tough sell.*"

"E-talk?"

"Executive BS." She didn't care if she was being rude, she was tired of this whole discombobulation of her career dream.

"When we first met I knew your art was what I needed to convince them."

"Is that why you kept close to me? Because you knew about the buy out? That after that happened I'd be desperate? Or should I say destitute? And you'd get a good deal?"

"Not at all. I enjoy your company, Marcie. Very much. I want you to be part of this project, and I hope you'll want to do it. I didn't know the buy out would happen so soon. My grandfather led us to believe he was still months away from even approaching the heirs of C&B. I wanted to see you successful. Then, when your obligation with Caledon and Bishops was finished, I was going to invite you to work with me." He reached out and covered her hand with his.

Marcie was touched by his sincerity, but disappointed. She wanted to be part of his life, not just his project.

"I did the *Himalayan Odyssey* book for my father," Greg said and Marcie could see the pain in his eyes. His hand still held hers, his thumb rubbing lightly over the top of her wrist in warm circles. "But I'm not here to talk about the past. I'm here because you have given me a new and exciting future. This project is mine. I want to prove to myself and my family that I have what it takes to carry the business successfully into the future. But I'm earthbound enough to know I need someone like you. I need *you* to make it work. I can see us working together for years to come. It could be ours, if you'll join me."

"You're very persuasive. You make me want to join you and you don't even have a consensus from your family." Right now, sitting across the table from her, looking so hopeful, even vulnerable—as though he'd never realize his dream without her—she was ready to go anywhere with him. But she wouldn't let him off that easily. ***

***

Greg was feeling frustrated. He wanted to make things right for Marcie; he wanted to make up for the lies and half-truths. His grandfather was right, he was immature. But if she wanted a good licensing contract he wanted to give her the best. "I'm sorry this hasn't worked out for you, but I'm sure I can make it happen."

She looked at him with a sad, resigned expression that cut him to the core.

"You don't believe me, do you? You don't trust me." It was his own fault. His grandfather was right, he was immature. "What can I say or do to prove to you I *will* make this happen for you?"

"I want to trust you, but there are some things…"

"Like what? Give me a chance to explain. That's all I ask."

She hesitated, wiping up the last of her egg with the last of her toast. "When you returned from Glasgow you said you met with Mr. Fairmont. He was in Edinburgh." Her disillusioned expression crushed him.

"You're right. I lied. I have no excuse except I wanted to delay you finding out that your contract was in jeopardy. I thought I could spare you more pain. Obviously, it's had the opposite effect. What else?"

"No offense, but I want a licensing agreement with an established licensing company."

"McInnis House Press has been licensing images for sixty years. We have a wide range of manufacturers we contract with. Any other reasons?"

"My visa became void when my contract with Caledon became void. I think I'm illegal."

"I can handle the visa. What else?"

She worried her thumbnail with her teeth and he reached to pull her hand away. She smiled unselfconsciously, and he realized, as his heart constricted, that he loved her. And what the hell was he going to do about that?

***

After breakfast, on their way to the car, Greg took Marcie's hand in his. "I'll convince my grandfather, you can count on it."

"Okay." It was all Marcie could say. She should feel grateful that someone in a successful publishing company thought so highly of her work, but somehow it fell flat. She wanted her career dream as much as ever, but she wanted Greg to want her, too.

"Let's go home, Marcie."

"Why, Greg? What's in Inverness for me?" She wanted him to say he was in Inverness for her. But she knew he wasn't ready. Not until he moved from considering her a business venture to considering her his destiny.

"We discussed this at breakfast."

"But nothing's certain, is it? Meanwhile, I have a dozen publishers I need to contact in Glasgow."

"It will happen. I have more than my own goals to work for now. I have yours, too. When we get home, let me use some of your watercolors in my proposal. It's the only way they'll see what I've seen. It's the only way they'll understand the vision."

"All right." Was she making a mistake going home with him when she should be pounding the pavement in Glasgow?

**

The drive *home* to Inverness was enjoyable. Marcie happily listened as Greg talked about all his ideas. He was pleased and impressed when she added her own suggestions. She was beginning to feel that this just might happen. Her career, anyway.

He seemed more confident than the first time he'd talked to her about it. He seemed… content. In fact, he seemed happy. She wondered if she was the reason or if it was because he was getting her art.

When he pulled up in front of Judy's cottage, Marcie felt as if she'd come home.

Greg walked with her to the door, carrying her bags. He unlocked the door and set her bags in the hall. "I'm sorry to set you down and leave, but there's a backlog waiting for me at the office. Here's the phone you left behind. I'll call later."

Marcie took it, feeling her cheeks heat at the embarrassment of how she'd left without waiting for an explanation from Greg.

"I'm so glad you're home," he said. He pulled her into his arms, kissed her, then left.

Marcie stood in Judy's hall wondering what he'd meant. Confused, she picked up her bags. Dafydd had returned from his visit to Wales, so she no longer had a room of her own. She piled her things in a corner of the living room and went looking for Rumbles. Even without a room of her own she had returned home, to her *home*.

***

The day after she returned to Inverness she gathered her supplies and walked to the river. Her exercises now included drawing and some painting. She wanted to paint something for Greg, and hoped she would be able to do it well enough for him to see she was improving quickly. She was still far from her pre-accident skill but she could tell she would get there. She could feel the connection between her brain and her fingers growing stronger every day.

She sat on a bench with the view of the buildings across the River Ness and began to pencil in the scene. When the light was just as she wanted, she took several reference photos. It would take her a while to finish the watercolor and she didn't want to depend on her memory when she was back at Judy's finishing it.

It took time and careful concentration but she worked all evening and was happy with the results. It wasn't her best but was more than she'd thought she'd be doing four weeks after injuring her arm.

All the time she worked on the painting she thought of Greg and wondered what he really felt for her. Was he afraid to risk his heart? He'd lost someone close to him not too long ago. It must be difficult to take that chance again. But she was patient. She just hoped she had enough time left in Scotland to wait for him to realize he was in love with her.

***

When Greg arrived at work after taking Marcie home, Judy followed him to his office. "I just talked to Marcie. I don't think she's going to be comfortable at the cottage. I think she feels like she's in the way now that Dafydd is home."

"Do you want her to stay in some sterile hotel or lonely bed and breakfast?"

"No. Surely your reno is near completion?"

"Aye, it is. But as tempting as it is to have Marcie in my home, I don't think Granddad or Rowan would take me or my proposal seriously if they knew she was living with me. I wasn't exactly known for my restraint with women when I was younger." He grabbed the sack Judy had left on his desk and took out a scone. "Give it a few more days. I'll find something suitable for her."

Seemingly satisfied, she didn't comment.

"Will you draw up a standard McInnis House Press agreement for Marcie?" He took a bite of scone. "Delicious, you make the best." But he remembered Marcie's scones.

"How do I draw a contract for illustrations when all we do is photography?"

"You're clever, figure it out. I've got the hard part: convincing Old Gregor and Rowan to accept it."

Greg took the watercolors Marcie lent him to the art department and asked Anna to set them in a presentation folio. While he waited, he called his grandfather and uncle and arranged a meeting for lunch in Fort William the following day. The next few hours he spent contacting a caterer and catching up with the piles on his desk christy olesen

170

Highland sheep

CHAPTER TWELVE

Greg drove to Fort William with Marcie's watercolors and samples of published illustrated journals on the seat beside him. He felt confident today would be the day McInnis House Press would start something new and fresh.

He met with Old Gregor and Uncle Rowan over lunch in the dining room at Mòirneas. The caterer had prepared, delivered and served a midday meal of their favorites.

They talked as they ate, Greg expounding on the advantages of expanding their illustration resources, the others always falling back on great-grandfather's vision.

" 'Keep tae the fore,' Father always said." Old Gregor shook his fist in the air as though he led a military charge. "It means stay modern, stay in touch with technology; daena get easy-oasy wi' yer goods."

"If I recall," Greg said, "he was also known to say, *'Gie fowk whit thay want, e'en if thay daena ken whit thay want.'* Give folk what they want, even if they don't know what they want_."

chRisty olesen

"I know what it means," Old Gregor said then looked at Rowan, who was the reason Greg had translated.

"Obviously, you're set on changing the direction of MHP," Rowan said. "Perhaps you're ready to set off on your own. Why not take over C&B? Then you can do as you please." A not-so-subtle hint that if Greg left MHP, Rowan wouldn't mind. He'd then have sole control of the business after Gregor IV retired. That was something Greg didn't want to see as long as there was a willing McInnis around.

"I am not set on changing the direction of MHP, only broadening the scope a bit. And I certainly have no desire to leave McInnis House. I wish to see it prosper and keep up with the industry, just as great-grandfather intended."

"Well said, me laddie." Old Gregor reached and slapped Greg's shoulder. "Well said. You're a McInnis. You belong here." His grandfather turned a frown on Rowan.

Greg: one. Rowan: zero.

Rowan tried again. "C&B is the perfect vehicle for your ideas. You can hire new talent, people who share your vision."

"C&B will continue as is," Old Gregor said. "Its strength is in its serious, technical guide books and maps. Their Monroe series is worth the price we paid for the company. We'll not corrode that reputation with prissy little books filled with fidgety little watercolors."

Greg: two. Rowan: zero.

Sort of.

Greg could feel the heat rise up his neck. "*They've* been publishing such for years. They publish art books as well as guide books. I see no reason why we can't do the same." Greg needed to change his grandfather's concept of painted illustration. He came needing to convince both his grandfather and his uncle that his ideas were grounded in economic fact, and he came prepared to do just that.

"Show us, Greg." His grandfather sat forward, stabbing the table with his fork for emphasis, adding another mark to its history. "Show us something to get excited about. Demonstrate what excites you."

That was the Gregor McInnis Greg knew and loved: the man who could consider something outside his own experience, if only after gnawing an old bone and finding no nutrition.

"Let's take a break," Greg said. "The caterers will clear the table, then I'll present my ideas." He stood and crossed the room to where he'd left his samples.

How do you communicate a feeling, an intuition, a vision? He was usually the one who had to be convinced. The editors and art directors came to him when they had new ideas, new talent to present. When he'd organized the Himalaya expedition he would have had to convince his grandfather and uncle to agree to it, but he'd chosen to keep it a secret. The project was something he would have done with or without their approval. At that time he had thought it would be easier without Granddad or Rowan knowing.

He remembered the Grace Hopper quote he'd framed and hung on his office wall when planning the expedition: *If it's a good idea, go ahead and do it. It's much easier to apologize than it is to get permission.*

His current ideas were not a one-time publication; they would be ongoing, for as long as Marcie wanted to be part of it. It might even go beyond Marcie. There would be room for other artists he would discover, those he and Marcie would discover together. Today it would be easier to ask permission, to sell the concept.

As the caterers cleared the table, leaving a dish filled with tempting, bite-sized cakes and chocolates—Gregor's weakness— Greg arranged his samples, published illustrated journals and books, most done with watercolor.

He opened the presentation folder Anna had made for Marcie's watercolors. They looked even more incredible in tidy mats and acetate covers. A note fluttered to the floor, he picked it up and read it.

Greg, whatever decision your people make, I appreciate all you've done for me. Marcie

Greg looked up at his grandfather and uncle, who were choosing decadent tidbits from the tray of confections on the table, and he knew his dream, but more importantly, Marcie's dream, was about to come true.

***

After driving back to Inverness, Greg sat at his desk and looked at Marcie's watercolors. He'd taken each matted art piece and leaned one against his computer monitor, another against the in-out box, and the third against the lamp.

Old Gregor and Rowan had been hesitant at first, but then Greg had seen their expressions change as they'd studied the images. The sample books had helped to prove to both men that yes, indeed, other publishers printed 'fussy' books with artists' illustrations. Only these weren't fussy. Greg's samples covered a large spectrum of styles from impressionistic to realistic.

Eventually his grandfather had agreed this was something they needed to consider. Rowan finally agreed when he realized he was the odd man out. It had been decided that Greg would write a proposal, then, because it was new to McInnis House Press, they'd meet again to discuss it.

Greg's proposal had already been written. He'd started it the year before and had finished it with renewed anticipation the day he'd met Marcie.

"Let's discuss it now," he'd said, and handed each man a neat folder.

***

At the end of the day, in his empty house, Greg opened his mobile phone and hit the number of the phone he'd given back to Marcie.

"Hello, Greg," she said with a seductive note in her voice he hadn't heard before.

"How did you know it was me?"

"You always think I'm psychic." She laughed. "The phone has caller ID."

He wasn't prepared for the effect of hearing her voice or her laugh. She probably didn't know what it did to him. It made him stupid, for one thing. "Of course." He wanted to be there with her, not across town in his empty house. "How are you?"

"Fine. And you?"

"Good." He sat back and put his feet up on his father's desk, crossed at the ankle. "I gave the proposal today."

"Oh, good. How'd it go?" Her voice sounded expectant.

"Very well."

"I imagine you're used to giving proposals. I'd have been a nervous wreck."

"That's why you do what you do and I do what I do." He laughed. It came easily now. It felt good. "I never saw two men change their point of view so quickly."

"I guess that means they liked your presentation." Her voice was lighter, brighter.

"Aye. But it was your watercolors that sold them." He dropped his feet to the floor, and turned to look out the window in the direction of Judy's neighborhood. "I should have a contract for you soon. After I catch up with a few things, I'll pick you up in the afternoon. We'll celebrate."

"You're very certain."

"That I am." He sat up. "Marcie, thank you for lending me the watercolors. They made all the difference in presenting my ideas."

"You're welcome."

They talked a while longer until Greg heard voices in the background. "Sounds like Judy and Dafe are home."

"Yes. I'm cooking dinner for them."

"I won't keep you then. I'll see you tomorrow."

"I'm looking forward to it. Good night, Greg."

"Good night, sweetheart."

***

The next morning Marcie walked to the shops with a lighter step than the last time she'd been there. Greg had called her sweetheart. Did he even know he had?

Pleasantly tired after her walk, Marcie sat before the small computer, which sat where she'd left it in Judy's lounge. She booted it up and opened her email inbox.

```
Marcie,
     There hasn't been a decision yet on
that job at the middle school. There's still
time to apply. Just let me know if you're
coming home as planned, and I'll meet you at
the airport.
     Dad
```

Hi Dad.
I plan to stay until the last of June.
My tickets are for San Francisco, not Reno,
so don't worry about picking me up. Thanks
anyway.
MW

MerciMe! Girl,
You are a traveling fool. I just caught
up with your emails. Gawd, I'd love to see
Edinburgh. How long are you going to be
there?
Sounds like you're doing well with your
physical therapy. Keep it up.
I ran into Joel the other day. He said
he was about to put your stuff in storage!
Gotta go, on call tonight.
Wallie, MD!

Wallie, hi.
I'm back in Inverness. Maybe someday we
can do Edinburgh together. Maybe even London!
If you see Joel tell him that's ok. I
don't have much, but I'd rather it was out of
his way.
Love ya. Marcie

Marcie,
Jeff and I are going to buy tickets to
Edinburgh and come see you! Surprise! You do
have a spare bed, don't you? We'll go see a
show. Is *Cats* still playing? Or that one
about the sewers of Paris? Can you pick us up
at the airport?
Later, kiddo. Mom.

MOM! STOP! DON'T BUY TICKETS TO
EDINBURGH! I'M NOT THERE! I'm back in
Inverness. I'm staying at Judy's and there is
no spare bed. If you still want to go to
Edinburgh, I highly recommend it.
XX Marcie.

Marcie.

Saw your friend Wallie. Says your deal over there has fallen through. If you can be in New York by Wednesday, I've set up a meeting for you with Amanda Roth. Joel.

christy olesen

Inverness, along the River Ness

CHAPTER THIRTEEN

In the afternoon, when Greg felt he had caught up enough with the backlog on his desk, he called his grandfather to find out if he and Rowan had made a decision.

"Confound-it, boy. You don't give a man time to think, let alone make a sane decision."

"I want to sign Ms. Winters before she returns to the States." It wasn't a lie this time. Marcie planned to return home as scheduled. He needed a reason to keep her from leaving, like a firm contract with McInnis House Press.

"You know, Son, at first I thought it might have been a mistake letting you take over your father's position. I thought you were too young and inexperienced. You seemed so young when you were thirty and I was looking at you from eighty. But I didn't have the heart to deny you so soon after you lost your father. And so soon after losing my son, I didn't have the heart to send you off on any more remote photo expeditions. I wanted you close. I wanted you safe.

"I'll admit I was very upset when I found out about the trip to the Himalayas. But I wouldn't have expected anything less from you. You are your father's son and I've always been proud of both

179

of you. I've always envied your ability to take on tough physical tasks, to travel to difficult locations for photo shoots, to put up with the discomforts of traveling in foreign countries.

"I believe now that you'll fill your father's shoes rather well." Old Gregor's voice was thick with emotion, and it took Greg several beats before he could trust his own voice.

"Think I'm grown up enough?" Greg teased to ease the tension.

"You're well on your way to downright maturity. There's a difference between grown up and being mature, you know."

"Tell me." Greg sat back. Maybe he had matured; he was enjoying talking to his grandfather, man to man, as peers. It wasn't a conference; they were having a conversation.

"Grown up means you show up on time, complete your assignments, pay your bills and taxes, don't get pissed and drive." The old man cleared his throat. "Maturity means you take responsibility, you do a job you don't necessarily want to do because it needs to be done and others are counting on you. You consider the welfare of others and you stand up for what you believe in."

Greg was stunned.

"You still there, lad?"

Greg felt his own throat tighten. "Yes, sir. Thank you for the vote of confidence."

"Aye, well, when I was twenty-five I persuaded your great-grandfather to publish a set of children's books, illustrated with watercolors."

"No! I don't believe it." Greg laughed.

"Aye, it's true. I'll leave them to you when I die. They're still in the attic here at Mòirneas. I'd be too embarrassed to show them to you now. I have quite a few left. They didn't sell very well."

"I'm sorry."

"It was a good experience, just the same. Yours will sell better."

"Mine?" Greg barely got the word out.

"Aye, go ahead and sign the girl. And bring her around soon. I want to meet her."

"I will. Thank you, Granddad."

"My pleasure, Son."

***

Several introspective moments after he hung up, Greg lifted the phone to call Marcie with the good news, then changed his mind and put the receiver down again. This he had to tell her in person. He wanted to see her excitement at regaining her dream. He wanted the occasion to be special. He tidied his desk and took his outgoing mail into Judy's office.

"What's happened? You look right pleased with yourself."

"Let you know tomorrow. I have a date to keep," he said as he went through the door.

He heard Judy call after him. "A date? With whom?"

"Tomorrow," he called back.

On his way down the stairs, he called his favorite restaurant. He was excited. Excited for Marcie, for himself, for the future. Their future. He couldn't help the smile that tugged at his lips as he slipped into the Rolls and pulled out into afternoon traffic. He stopped at home to change, gathered a few things, then set off in the Land Rover to see Marcie. He couldn't wait to see her face when he told her that her project was a go.

***

Marcie stared at Joel's email. What was he trying to do? Tear her apart? Just when Greg's company was so close to picking up her project, just when it looked as if she'd have a good reason to stay in Scotland, Joel was tempting her with Amanda Roth? *The* Amanda Roth, top artists' agent? And so businesslike, so unemotional. No '*How have you been?*' No '*Sorry about the accident that almost ended your career before it began.*'

So she was straight to the point in her reply. No '*How have you been?*' No '*Why did you dump me like last week's garbage?*'

        Joel.
        Is this for real? Amanda Roth? The
    Amanda Roth? How certain is this?
        M.W.

Marcie paced Judy's lounge hoping Joel was on-line. Maybe she should call him. But she couldn't bring herself to do it. She didn't want to hear his voice. She didn't want the past butting into her new present.

Amanda Roth was legendary, the holy grail of agents for artists. Could Marcie trust Joel to have gotten a bonafide appointment? Could she do the work Ms. Roth would expect? Yeah, she was healing, improving, but how long would it take before she was back to what she'd been before the accident? Would it be bogus to sell herself using her previous work? Shouldn't she sell herself with samples of what she could do now? How would she be able to put together a portfolio in such a short time? The best she'd done so far was the scene of Inverness for Greg. But that was personal; she didn't want to use it for business. She hadn't given it to Greg yet and didn't want anyone else to see it before him. And she didn't want to give it to him then borrow it back to take it to New York. How tacky would that be?

Greg had promised her a contract. Several times. But she hadn't seen it yet. Would he be able to convince the others in his company to accept it?

Even if McInnis House Press came through, she could still have an agent. It was good business sense to have an agent. In fact, it was imperative to get the jobs she wanted.

She continued to pace, and chewed on her thumbnail.

The computer dinged and Marcie almost knocked it off the table in her rush to open the reply.

```
Marcie.
It's for real. You'll have to go
through preliminary approval before Amanda
will see you. Can you make it?
J.
```

Marcie bit her lower lip and answered.

```
Joel.
Give me 24 hours to make arrangements.
I'll let you know.
MW
```

She didn't hit the send button. *Don't look too eager.* Then she heard someone knock on the door, and a key in the lock.

***

Greg knocked several times with no answer before he pulled out Judy's spare key and unlocked the front door. The chain was on. "Marcie? It's Greg." Relief dissipated the feeling of *déjà vu* as he remembered a fortnight ago when he'd come to see Marcie and found her gone. At least the chain on meant she was home. Just not answering his knocks.

"Come in," she called from the depths of the house.

"Chain's on."

"Right. Of course. Sorry." Her voice became clearer as she approached. "Hold on." She pushed the door shut before he even had a look at her, and his urge to see her was strong enough he would have broken the chain if he'd had to. He heard the chain drop. "Come in," she said as she backed up, opening the door wide. He wanted to take her in his arms and swing her around in the air, only there wasn't room in Judy's hall, and she looked distracted. As though he could have been anyone at the door.

"Hello, Marcie. You're settled in?" It was a daft thing to say, but he had trouble reading her. She wasn't her bright, cheerful self. Not the woman with the shining smile he'd brought home with him from Edinburgh that morning.

"Would you like something to drink? I was just making some iced tea."

"Sounds good." She could offer him apple cider vinegar and he'd take it.

She motioned to the lounge. "Have a seat, I'll be right back."

He watched her walk to the kitchen before he entered the lounge. He was too excited to sit, so he perused Judy's bookshelves. She kept family memorabilia among the books. Photos. Small, unrecognizable, objects d'art made by Dafe. A collection of small wooden boxes, which probably held the little treasures of her life.

A ruckus from the back of the house announced the arrival of Judy and her son. Greg stepped out into the hall, happy to see Dafe.

"Uncle Greg! Look what I made." Dafe held out a sheet of construction paper covered with dinosaurs cut from vivid colors of more paper.

"Clever boy! Where will you display it?"

"Here." Dafe ran into the lounge and Greg followed. Dafe propped his art against the books on a shelf he could barely reach. "There. Looks good, doesn't it?"

"Aye. What else did you do today?"

"We did computers. Most of the kids did Gaelic language games but they let me do Welsh. I learned some more words. I can't wait 'til Granpa calls." Dafe spied the little computer on the table where Marcie had left it open.

It crossed Greg's mind that maybe news from home had caused Marcie to look shaken when he'd come in. He didn't want to snoop, but he wanted to know what had caused the light to dim in her beautiful eyes, what had caused her distressed expression before she'd hid it from him by rushing to the kitchen. Maybe he could help.

"I know how to do this. Look, Uncle Greg." Dafe pounced on the computer.

Greg crossed the room in two strides to stop the boy from touching the keys. There was an unsent email on the screen and Greg didn't want him to accidentally send it off before Marcie was ready.

Dafe's attention was caught by his mother's call and he pulled away from Greg and ran to her.

Marcie was taking a long time in the kitchen. He saved the open email to drafts, shut down the laptop, closed it and stuck it on a high shelf away from little boy's fingers.

As he passed Judy's room he saw her sitting on her bed with her son under her arm as he showed her something cradled in his hand. It was a tender scene of parental love and sharing, and he wondered if he'd waited too long to realize he wanted that, too.

Marcie stood in the middle of the kitchen, staring, chewing on her thumbnail. He gently pulled her hand from her mouth. "What's wrong, Marcie?"

"I can't remember if you said cola or lemon-lime."

"You offered iced tea, but it doesn't matter. Something's upset you."

"It's nothing." She seemed to snap to and busied herself with the tea. "Do you like it sweet? With lemon? Dafe likes both, so does Judy. They're home."

"Yes, I noticed." He looked at the curlicue iron chairs of Judy's bistro set and decided to remain standing. "Put some of that in a flask and we'll take it with us."

"To the living room?" She looked at him as if he were from another planet.

"We're going out." He began to look in Judy's cabinets for a container.

"We're going out?"

He found what he was looking for, shooed her off to change into something casual and warm.

"At least tell me where we're going."

"The longest day of the year has passed. The days are growing rapidly shorter, so let's enjoy the late sun while we can."

"Oh shoot! That's something I wanted to do while I was in Scotland, stay out late on the longest day of the year. You remembered." Now she looked at him as if he were a god and he wanted to bottle his sense of fulfillment.

"Go on, change." He shooed her out of the kitchen.

While she changed he stepped to Judy's door. When she looked up, he said, "Marcie and I are going out. Don't wait up."

"Have a good time." Judy turned back to her son but not before giving Greg an encouraging smile.

***

When Marcie finished changing she found Greg at the front door with the thermos of iced tea. He looked outstanding in worn blue jeans and an oatmeal cable-knit pullover. She grabbed her bag and dropped in her camera. "Will this do?" She'd put on jeans and a ghost walk T-shirt he'd bought her in Edinburgh.

"Perfect. Grab a cardi and a raincoat. Are those the only shoes you have?"

"Yes. Shoes are important?" She looked down at her worn tennies.

"Shoes are always important in Scotland. We'll be walking in some rough country. But if it's all you have… then I guess I might have to carry you."

Marcie was still trying to lower her temperature when Greg opened the door of the Land Rover and Bobby jumped into her arms. "Bobby's going with us? Now will you tell me where we're going?" She buckled herself in and waited for an answer.

Greg didn't speak but he had the cutest mischievous expression. She'd never seen him really enjoying himself before. He'd always seemed to be touched by sadness, even when they had been having a good time together. But now, he was different. His good mood was infectious.

Bobby was excited and kept turning in her lap, first to look out the window then to lick her chin. He made her giggle, or was it the prospect of an evening out, a surprise evening out, with Greg all to herself, away from business, that made her giddy?

They drove through Inverness and soon Greg stopped at the valet of an expensive-looking restaurant.

"We're not going in here, are we? I'm not dressed right."

A valet walked up to Greg's window, Greg gave his name and the man walked away. He returned in a few minutes with a large box, walked around to the back of the car, opened the hatch and placed the box inside. When he came to the window Greg handed him something and they drove away.

"What was that all about?" She twisted in her seat to look back at the restaurant. It was impressive. She was a little disappointed they weren't going to dine there. But she was excited, wondering what his surprise would be.

They headed southeast out of Inverness, a direction Marcie hadn't been. She watched the scenery change from city to suburb to open country. They passed by farmland, meadows, small lochs and rising mountains. After turning west, Marcie could see the high mountains of the Highlands ahead. The road climbed and zigzagged until Greg turned on to a dirt road. He parked the car at the edge of a meadow, shut off the engine, then turned in his seat to face her.

"This is beautiful," Marcie said. A sap-green forest surrounded the meadow; wild flowers grew among the grasses. So many colors Marcie lost count. "Are we having a picnic here? It's perfect."

"Not here. Up there." He pointed to a ridge above the treetops.

"Oh, up there." It looked awfully high. But Greg wouldn't take her someplace where she would be in danger or frightened. "Okay."

heR scoccish ceo

He was already out of the car and opening her door. He took Bobby and let him down to explore the meadow. "Take a look around while I get our things together."

Marcie walked into the tall grasses to get a closer look at the wildflowers. She recognized several from her research before coming to Scotland. Yellow buttercup, red clover, and violets. Several thistles, a symbol of Scotland. Wild strawberry and vetch—a wild sweat pea. She took some photos but wanted to sit right down and paint them all.

A sharp whistle startled her and she looked up. Without realizing it, she'd crossed the meadow. Greg stood near his car and waved her to come back. Bobby, who had followed her, was already bounding through the tall grasses to his master.

Greg had donned a hefty backpack and held out a smaller one for her. It wasn't heavy and she guessed it held their raincoats. A picnic blanket was rolled and tied underneath. She looped her bag over her shoulder then shrugged into the back pack as Greg held it for her.

"You'll be all right with this?" he asked.

"Yep. I've backpacked before. Yours looks heavy though." Plus he had his big camera around his neck.

"Only going up. It will be lighter coming down."

"It's our picnic? From that restaurant? I can't wait to see what they've made for us."

For the first twenty minutes it was an easy uphill walk through the fir forest. Dark, quiet and cool. The fragrance of summer was in the air: the pitchy scent of the pines, warmed earth, wildflowers. Birds chittered to each other from tree to tree. Midges buzzed.

Bobby was left to wander as he pleased, but called back to the trail by his master's whistle when he wandered too far off.

As they left the forest the trail steepened, cutting through brush and heather. Marcie stopped to pick a sprig and put it behind her ear.

They stopped to share a drink from the thermos of iced tea. She kept up with Greg for several minutes before something caught her eye, some lichen on a large rock. Its colors and structure fascinated her. She took close-up photos of several formations. Greg took pictures of her taking pictures of rocks and they both laughed.

The trail began to cross rocky ground and the land fell away on either side. Marcie could see the ridge ahead. It rose like the fin of a shark out of a sea of firs. It looked rugged and she welcomed the challenge. She walked to the edge and looked over onto the tops of the forest. She wanted to get over the fear of heights she'd experienced since her accident. When she turned back to the trail Greg was there, waiting for her, frowning.

"I'm sorry. Have I done something wrong?"

"It's not a good idea to stand so close to the edge. The rocks are loose; you could lose your footing. I thought Judy said you're afraid of heights."

"I am. But this is not a straight drop. It will help me get over my fear if I face it."

They walked on a little further. A large bird flew low over their heads and landed in a treetop below them. Marcie went to the edge to get a better look. "Was that an eagle?"

"Good God, woman! Stay away from the edge. You're taking years off my life."

"I wish I had binoculars. Then maybe I could tell if it's an eagle."

"It's an osprey, and come back to the trail. Please."

She did, smiling at his concern.

When they reached the top and laid down their packs, Marcie marveled at the sight before her. Even though they hadn't climbed to the top of a mountain, the view was spectacular: mountain range after mountain range, some still clinging to their winter snow in the last days of June.

Greg pointed out Ben Nevis in the distance. "We're in the Monadhliath Mountains, about halfway between Inverness and Fort William, south of Loch Ness."

"It's breathtaking. What's in the other direction?"

"Glens and lochs and small villages."

Wind started to buffet them and Marcie folded her arms against the chill. She wanted more than anything to kiss Greg, here, on top of the world. It wasn't Everest, but it was probably the closest she'd get. The thought made her tremble.

Greg found a sheltered spot and laid out the picnic blanket. Then Marcie helped him unload his backpack, which wasn't a hiker's backpack at all but an insulated picnic pack with cutlery, plates, wine glasses and cloth napkins, all coordinated in a blue and green plaid reminiscent of his tartan tie. There was even a little cutting board. After Greg sliced narrow baguettes and cheese, they piled on their plates what they wished from several containers the restaurant had filled for them. Roast beef, smoked salmon, rustic breads, mustards, cheeses and fruit.

"Scrumpy?" Greg asked before opening the bottle, obviously remembering the first time Marcie had tried it.

"Yes, today I will have scrumpy."

He poured and touched his glass to hers. "To you, Marcie. May all your dreams come true."

"And to you, Greg, for your kindness, generosity and help, without which I'd probably be sitting in a tiny cabin in Center City licking my wounds."

He laughed and she thought it was the first time she'd heard him genuinely laugh; she hoped it wouldn't be the last.

Bobby accepted gourmet tidbits as if he were starving, then curled up on a tuft of grass and fell asleep.

After they packed away the picnic things, Greg moved to sit back against a rock and motioned for Marcie to join him. She obliged, snuggled in close and he put his arm around her.

"It's more sheltered from the wind here," he said. "Still warm from the sun. We'll have a good view of the sunset in a few hours. Do you still want to wait for it?"

"Yes." She pulled the picnic blanket over their legs. "That was a delicious dinner. The crab salad was heaven. This is a gorgeous spot to spend the almost-longest day of the year. An all-around wonderful surprise. Thank you."

"You're welcome." He pulled her a little closer.

Given the romantic evening, the dreamer in Marcie wanted to hear a declaration of love, plans for a future together; but the realist knew it was too soon. Just because she'd fallen for him didn't mean he felt the same for her. But she would enjoy the evening and treasure it.

"You were upset when I arrived at Judy's. Anything I can help you with?"

She hesitated, not knowing if she should tell him. He'd already done so much for her. Could she ask him for more? But she valued his opinion and his advice. "Do you know Amanda Roth?"

"She's a big-time agent in New York. I know of her. I've never met her or done business with her. Why?"

"Joel—that's the guy I use to... um... know when I lived in San Francisco—he's made an appointment for me to meet Ms. Roth." She moved away from Greg so she could face him, read his expressions. She moved onto her knees and sat back on her heels. "But I don't think I'm ready yet. I mean, I'm doing much better than I thought I would by this time but I don't know how long it's going to take before I'm back to where I was before the accident. If I keep the appointment, do I take the watercolors I did before the accident or do I take the ones I've done since? And if I take the ones I've done since, how will she see what I will be able to do when I'm completely recovered?"

"Whatever level of recovery you are at, you need to show her what you're doing now. Otherwise you'll be misrepresenting yourself. It could jeopardize your relationship with her." He paused and she didn't like that the touch of sadness had returned to his eyes. "You could wait until you're fully recovered."

"That could be months. And an appointment with Ms. Roth might not come again."

"If you're not at your best now, she might not be interested."

Marcie pulled her bag close and pulled out several small watercolors. "This is what I've done recently." She handed them to him. "Do you think they're good enough to show her?"

He looked at each one carefully, his expression showing surprise, even delight, then resignation as he handed them back. "They're exceptional. I think you should keep the appointment."

She tilted her head and looked at him. "What about you? What about McInnis House Press? Has your family made a decision?"

"That doesn't matter now. You should go see Ms. Roth. But it's your decision, Marcie. I want you to do what's best for you."

He looked a little defeated then. He expected her to pick Amanda Roth over him? It tore at her heart to see him ready to give up his dream so she could go with Ms. Roth. But it also angered her that he would give up without fighting for her or his own dream.

"Signing with Ms. Roth doesn't mean I can't sign with McInnis House Press."

"Ms. Roth can find an agreement that's more lucrative than MHP can afford. Isn't that what you want? The best licensing contract you can get? Amanda Roth can provide that. With McInnis House Press you'd be starting somewhere in the middle. With Amanda, you'll be launched to the top. She has an unblemished record for doing just that for talented artists. I want you to consider all your options, what's best for you, for your career."

After weeks of wanting to offer her a contract he was now asking her to consider *all* her options? It was his dream as much as hers. "What are all my options? Is a contract with McInnis House Press one of them?"

"I have convinced my grandfather and uncle to use your illustrations in books as well as licensed items. So, yes, McInnis House Press is one of your options. But Amanda Roth will have more and better options for you to consider."

She ignored his comment about Ms. Roth and focused on what he had accomplished in his own company. "You persuaded your people to publish a book illustrated with watercolors? You didn't even know if I'd be able to paint as well as I used to before the accident."

"I believed you would."

"But you don't believe, now that I have an appointment with a top agent, that I'd want a contract with McInnis House Press."

"As I just said, Ms. Roth will have better options for you to consider. I want you to have the best. You're my proté—"

Marcie put a hand up to stop him. "I don't want to be your protégée. Don't get me wrong, I appreciate all you've done for me, and value your advice, but I've moved beyond that."

She stood then, and walked to the rim of their little plateau where she could look out over the glen below, and past the ridges of the mountains beyond. And think.

She chewed her thumbnail. Did she really want a contract with McInnis House Press? Or was it Greg McInnis she wanted? Was she really looking for a reason to stay in Scotland, to stay near Greg? She didn't need a contract with McInnis House Press to do that. She could work anywhere; that was the reason she was working for a licensing contract. That was what Ms. Roth could give her.

What she really needed—*really wanted*—was Greg to ask her to stay no matter what career path she chose. But would that happen?

She sighed heavily. Maybe she should forget Scotland, forget Greg, and fly to New York to meet Amanda Roth. It was a chance in a lifetime. She should grab it while the opportunity was available. But somehow she just couldn't muster the enthusiasm she would have a few weeks ago.

The wind increased, raced across the glen below her and rushed up and over the ridge. Clouds tore across the sky. They at least knew their direction. She was confused about her own. Again.

She heard Greg stand, step across the gravel, and stop behind her. Were his thoughts as mixed up as hers?

Marcie looked over the glen below, her arms folded. She faced the wind, which blew her hair around her face and took away the piece of heather tucked behind her ear.

Except for a narrow road hugging the base of the mountain and running its length, the glen below was wild and unspoiled. Forested areas mixed with barren land, some blushed with early heather. She wanted to be in Scotland in September when the hills were pink with heather in full bloom.

A small river snaked along the bottom of the valley. Marcie walked closer to the edge to look around a rocky protrusion. A flock of sheep ambled through the grasses, some wandering onto the road. The wind carried their bleats to her. They stopped, one or two heads rose to listen. Lambs ran among the sheep, playing tag with each other, climbing and jumping off small grassy hillocks. The scene was so quaint.

heR scottish ceo

More sheep raised their heads to listen, each facing up the glen. Marcie looked to see what had captured their attention. Something red flashed between the trees in the distance. A car. She edged closer to the drop-off, her fear forgotten in her panic for the sheep and lambs. She watched until the car came into sight again. It was a small sports car, moving fast. Too fast. She looked back at the sheep. Most were now on the road.

Her foot slipped in the gravel.

"Greg!"

***

Greg lunged and grabbed Marcie, pulling her away from the edge and into his arms before she slid further down the cliff. He held her tight, the fear of almost losing her pushing adrenalin through his veins like fire. The thundering of his heart nearly obscured the sheep's panicked bleats and the screeching tires and brakes below.

Then all was quiet. He raised one hand to cup the back of Marcie's head as tender feelings all but overwhelmed him. He'd almost lost her before he'd told her he loved her.

"Greg?"

He still held on tight, maybe too tight, but he couldn't let go. Not yet.

"Greg, what's wrong? "

He loosened his hold enough to allow her to tilt her head back to look at him.

"Greg? You're so pale. The sheep…"

"I thought… I'd lost you." His throat felt rough with emotion. "When you called my name in panic, I thought you were slipping over the cliff." He pulled her close again. "I can't lose you, Marcie. You're my world, my life." He pulled back again to look at her, blinked to clear his vision. "I realized it just now, in that split second when I thought I wouldn't reach you in time." He brushed a lock of windblown hair from her face. Her eyes sparkled with her own unshed tears. "I didn't think I had the emotional depth to love again, really love unconditionally. But I do. My love for you runs so deep I didn't recognize it until now. I love you, Marcie. Have I left it too late? Should I have said it sooner?"

"You're not too late. You're just in time."

christy olesen

He bent and kissed her, a gentle lingering kiss.
Reluctantly, he raised his head. "I think I have loved you since I
first looked into those eyes of yours, so full of wonder and trust.
Why else would I have followed you everywhere?"

"I thought you wanted my illustrations."

"That's what I told myself. I thought I needed your
artwork to inject life into my work, but I need you in my life. Sign
with me or sign with Ms. Roth, I don't care, as long as you stay.
Here. With me. In Inverness. I know I haven't been totally
honest—"

She touched a finger to his lips and giggled when he
captured it with his mouth. "I love you more than life. And I want
to sign with McInnis House Press." She reached up and kissed
him.

Having learned his lesson, Greg wasn't about to waste any
more time. He took Marcie's hands in his, then dropped to one
knee. He thought she'd had a bright smile before, but it paled in
comparison to the smile she gave him now.

"I don't have a ring, but I have a promise. I promise to
love you to the end of my days. Marry me, sweetheart."

She didn't hesitate. "Yes. I'll marry you, luv."

He rose, wrapped his arms around her and kissed her
soundly.

Bleats wafted up the ridge on the wind, and she pulled
away. "The sheep…? How many…?"

He looked over. "They got off the road in time."

She looked. "They're grazing as though nothing
happened."

But something *had* happened, just not to the sheep.
Something big. Something life changing. To him. To them.

"Sheep are not known for their brains," he said. Wind
whipped around them. "It's getting cold. Are you sure you want to
stay here until the sun sets?"

"I could stay here in the circle of your arms forever. Let's
stay until the sun rises."

Wildflowers

CHAPTER FOURTEEN EPILOGUE

Marcie stood in the vestibule of St. Bridget's, Judy and Gregor IV by her side. She had always wanted to be married on the longest day of the year, but after Greg had proposed to her, she hadn't wanted to wait a whole year.

"We could marry on December twenty-first," he'd said.

"The shortest day of the year?"

"Nae, the longest *night* of the year," he'd said, his eyes sparkling with mischief.

The setting sun would be shining through the church windows when she entered. It would be beautiful. But she wouldn't be looking at the windows.

Her father couldn't leave his job, so he'd said, even though Greg had offered to cover all his expenses. But Marcie was used to her parents' lack of interest. It didn't hurt as much as it had before she'd met her new family in Scotland. She felt more sorry for her father than herself. Her mother, on the other hand, had jumped at a chance for an all expenses paid trip for two to Scotland and had brought along her ski-instructor boyfriend and their skis.

Judy handed Marcie her bouquet. White rosebuds, pink heather and yellow freesia, then adjusted the Douglas-tartan sash pinned at her shoulder with a silver Celtic broach. Something borrowed, something blue. "We don't want it to cover your cleavage," Judy fussed, then winked. The sash crossed the bodice of her white satin and lace dress and was pinned at the hip in a bow in the style of an unmarried woman of the Highlands. At the reception she would change to the McInnis tartan and wear it on the other side, the sign of a married woman. *Soon she'd be a married woman!*

"Oh, Marcie," Judy said, "you look so beautiful. I'm going to cry before we even get up the aisle. I'm thrilled for you and Greg. I've never seen him so happy. After all he's been through... I just..." She kissed Marcie's cheek.

"Thank you, Judy. I'm pretty happy for us, too."

Greg's grandfather, who'd treated Marcie like a princess since the day they'd met, when he'd taken her hand and kissed it gallantly, took her arm and covered her hand with his. "The last time I walked a bride down the aisle I had thought it was a once-in-a-lifetime chance. And here I am again... a lucky man indeed."

"I never knew my grandfathers. I'm so happy to have one at last, and such a distinguished one. No one would ever know you're a big teddy bear."

Old Gregor laughed and, to Marcie's delight, blushed. Then he became serious. "He's a good man and he loves you." He squared his shoulders, faced the double doors and patted her hand. "Now, let's go and get you married. McInnis House needs an heir."

Marcie reached up and planted a lipstick kiss on his cheek. Nerves, excitement, anticipation danced through her like sunlight on rippling water.

Judy fiddled with the sash once more. "Ready? I hear our cue."

A Celtic arrangement of the wedding march with pipes and harp drifted through the vestibule doors. Marcie took a steadying breath, Old Gregor stood straighter, Judy pushed open the doors and they walked through.

Marcie saw only Greg and caught her breath. He stood near the altar, his eyes on her, his smile for her, his love shining.

He wore his green and blue tartan kilt—the same he'd been wearing the first time they'd met—and a short black coat fastened with large silver buttons at the bottom of the deep V of the lapels, and more buttons on the sleeves. A black vest over a crisp white shirt finished with a black bow tie. He had a long plaid pinned over his shoulder, draping front and back. His sporran was white fur with a silver clasp and chain. He seemed a different man, not the Greg in jeans and T-shirt or even Mr. McInnis in an impeccable business suit. Tonight he was Gregor McInnis VI, her Highland Chief.

Mark nodded to her from Greg's side, where he stood as best man, and winked. He wore all black with a black and red tartan kilt,. In Marcie's quick glance she noticed the black shirt under his casual suit coat was shiny. Just like Mark.

Before she reached Greg she looked around and saw her mother and Jeff, Wallie, and three more friends from college. They'd all come so far and Greg had made it possible. He'd wanted the church to be filled with her family and friends. They barely filled one pew, but they'd come to share her day.

She looked over to Greg's side of the church, and saw his mother—whom she'd met in October when she and Greg had visited her in British Columbia for Thanksgiving—and whom she adored. Greg's aunt and uncle, sister, brother-in-law, two nieces and a nephew, and tons of friends and business acquaintances filled the rest of the small chapel.

The ceilidh, a get-together and dance with friends and family, would follow the wedding and promised be great fun. She couldn't wait to give Greg the wedding gifts she'd made for him: the scene of Inverness across the river and another of the view from the ridge where he'd proposed and they'd spent their first night together. She'd completely recovered from her accident and had signed a three-year, exclusive contract with McInnis House Press. Her original project was finished and would be published as a hardcover book in time for the next tourist season.

Right now, she concentrated on the wedding ceremony. She'd remember it forever.

Old Gregor gave her away, his voice catching, and Greg

stepped up to take her hand. He placed a sprig of pink heather in the broach on her shoulder. Then they both faced the pastor, ready to begin their new life together.

The End

About the author/illustrator

Born and raised in L.A., romance writer Christy Olesen found a home in northern Nevada just over the hill from the Lake Tahoe, where the winters aren't as harsh, the tourist traffic isn't as heavy and the lifestyle isn't as hard to live up to. Christy has worked as a cashier, a parts packer for a model train company, an electronic circuit assembler, and as a dental laboratory ceramist She loves to read, garden, and travel the Sierra Nevada in a vintage 1955 travel trailer she restored herself.

Christy is also an accomplished watercolor artist and has worked as a model-home illustrator, free-lance illustrator, architectural illustrator, and is currently working as a graphic artist for a newspaper and magazine publisher in Carson City, Nevada.

Christy would love to hear from her readers and can be contacted at:
christy@christyolesen.com
http://christyolesen.com

Indie-Pendent Publishing Co.
http://www.indie-pendentpublishing.com

Cattle grazing on the shore of Loch Linnhe

heʀ scoᴛᴛιѕh ceo is also available as an ebook in full color, grayscale for black and white devices. Visit www.indie-pendentpublishing.com to find a link to the file for your device, or send as a gift.

Also available in ebook

Pet Rock Sex Manual, A Parody:
written and illustrated by Christy Olesen
PLEASE NOTE: THIS GRAPHIC
BOOKLET IS A PARODY AND NOT
INTENDED AS A BONA FIDE SEX
GUIDE. IT'S ALL IN FUN, SO HAVE FUN
AND ENJOY.
Approximately 19 pages.

Bonus material with this edition: A 1970s Fads, Hits and Fashions Trivia Test.

Perhaps the only sex manual rated G, this 14-page booklet was hand drawn and hand lettered in 1976. Pet Rocks were the latest fad during the 1975 Christmas gift-giving season and carried solid sales into 1976. After talking with friends about some of their high-maintenance pets, Gary Dahl conceived a "pet" that took no care or maintenance. His cleverly designed pet carrier packaging that enclosed a rock, some straw bedding and a manual sold millions.

While listening to a discussion on the radio about breeding pet rocks, Christy wanted to tell the commentators they were wrong. Their breeding methods would never work. So she wrote the PET ROCK SEX MANUAL, had it printed at a local copy shop and sold it for $2 to friends and family at a time when gas was 59¢ per gallon.
Take a trip back in time and have a chuckle with the PET ROCK SEX MANUAL. Available on Kindle, Nook and other ebook distributors.